He drew her to him and wrapped her in his embrace.

She rested her cheek against the lapel of his jacket, and he stood with her and soothed her until she quieted. He bent his head to her and kissed her, a feather-light kiss that brushed her lips and lit a fire within her. Her senses erupted in confusion. The warmth of his body caressed her, and comforted her, and his grey eyes meshed with hers as though he would see right into her soul. She wanted him to kiss her again, and she longed to lean on him, to have him shelter her from the brittle touch of life, but she was afraid. And she gazed at him with troubled eyes.

A&E DRAMA

Blood pressure is high and pulses are racing in these
fast-paced dramatic stories from Mills & Boon®
Medical Romance™. They'll move a mountain
to save a life in an emergency, be they the crash team,
emergency doctors, or paramedics. There are lots of
critical engagements amongst the high tensions
and emotional passions in these exciting stories
of lives and loves at risk!

Recent titles by the same author:

THE CONSULTANT'S SECRET SON
EMERGENCY AT THE ROYAL
IN HIS TENDER CARE

THE CONSULTANT'S SPECIAL RESCUE

BY
JOANNA NEIL

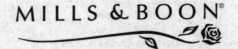

MILLS & BOON®

First published in Great Britain 2005
Harlequin Mills & Boon Limited,
Eton House, 18-24 Paradise Road, Richmond, Surrey TW9 1SR

© Joanna Neil 2005

ISBN 0 263 84336 X

Set in Times Roman 10½ on 12¼ pt.
03-1005-49483

Printed and bound in Spain
by Litografia Rosés, S.A., Barcelona

CHAPTER ONE

AMBER moved restlessly, trapped in a half-world between sleeping and waking. 'I'll find him for you, Mum,' she muttered. 'I'll find him.'

It was a troubled sleep, and somewhere in the back of her mind she knew that it was important that she wake up…there was something she had to do, wasn't there? But when she tried to open her eyes, her eyelids were heavy, as though they were weighted down, and her limbs felt like lead.

In the end the effort was all too much for her. She gave up the struggle.

If only the hammering would stop. It was there in the background, banging, banging—no, it was pounding in her head, clouding her mind, stopping her from thinking. She needed to think, to concentrate. There was something she had to do, but the continuous thump, thump refused to go away, and she couldn't clear her head enough to think what it was. Something to do with her brother, but it was all hazy in her mind.

Then there was a cracking sound, a shattering, and thankfully the banging at last stopped. She revelled in the peace, but not for long, because now there was another noise to take its place, an incessant droning sound that went on and on irritatingly.

Amber frowned. Her head hurt, and suddenly it was difficult to breathe. She started to cough, harsh, racking coughs that left her drained of energy.

'Come on,' a deep, masculine voice said. 'We have to go now.'

Amber paid him no attention. She wasn't going anywhere, no matter how authoritative the voice sounded. She was having enough trouble getting her eyes open, let alone even beginning to contemplate the thought of moving from this cosy bed. Was the man mad? And anyway, what was a man doing in her room?

She blinked, screwing up her eyes, and then finally managed to wrench them open. Looking around, she made a bleary survey of the room, and saw a dressing-table-cum-work surface and a chest of drawers. There was a chair, with some clothes draped over its back. She stared at them, and vaguely recognised the dress. Hadn't she'd been wearing that?

'I said we should go now.' It was the man's voice again, more demanding this time, as though he was beginning to lose patience. She decided to ignore it. There weren't any men in her life that had any say over what she did or didn't do and, besides, right now she was in no state to get up and go anywhere.

Another coughing spasm caught her unawares. Once it had passed, she tried to drag air into her lungs, but it was a struggle. What was happening to her? Was she ill? Her chest felt heavy, and every breath she took was laboured.

She stared about her once again. Where was she...? What was this place? It looked like students' accommodation, like a bedsit of some sort. What was she doing here?

Casting her mind back, she vaguely remembered a

party. Had she had too much to drink? Was that why she was feeling so out of sorts?

Suddenly, strong hands gripped her, and she realised that she was moving, that she was being lifted off the bed. Her eyes widened in shock, and she stared at those hands, at the powerful arms, and finally at the man they belonged to. His jaw was angular and hard boned, and his hair was black, crisp cut. His eyes bored into her, grey with a hint of blue, all-seeing and unrelenting. He was purposefully taking her away from where she had been comfortable and she resented his intrusion.

'Leave me alone,' she said tightly, aimlessly swatting at those imprisoning hands. 'Was it you who was doing all that banging while I was trying to sleep?' She broke off to cough and clear whatever it was that clogged her lungs. 'I don't want you here. Go away.'

She might as well not have spoken, because he didn't take any notice at all of her complaints. He simply pulled her up off the bed until she was in an upright position and she glared at him, her blue eyes sparking angrily.

Why was he here? She didn't know him. She had never seen him in her life before, but he seemed to tower above her, his whole image conveying strength and determination. How was she going to be able to fight him off?

Perhaps she could brace herself and use all her strength to resist him? A moment later her feet made contact with a rug, and somewhere in the back of her mind she had the idea that something was missing. She stared down at her feet and realised what was wrong. They were bare.

There was a faint sense of satisfaction in the discovery, because at least it meant that part of her brain was working. She tried to twist around, her gaze searching the floor.

'What are you looking for?'

'My shoes,' she started to say, but her voice sounded cracked and hoarse. She coughed, and tried again. 'Why are you still here?' She frowned, and then looked around again. 'I need my shoes.' A grey mist seemed to fill the room, at low level, grey, turning to black, and she couldn't see well enough to find them. Why was everything so difficult? This must all be a bad dream.

'We don't have time to look for them now.' He was urging her towards the door, a hand holding onto her arm, his other hand flat against the curve of her spine. She felt the heat of that touch as though he was stroking her bare flesh, and it was so vibrant a sensation, so intense that it seemed as though a solitary flame licked along her spine. She couldn't understand it. Why was she reacting to him this way?

His closeness propelled her into action. She tried to fight him, but it was no use, she was powerless against him.

'Here,' he said. 'Put this against your nose and mouth. It will keep the worst of the smoke away.' He handed her a large clean handkerchief and opened it over her face.

'What smoke?' she mumbled.

He didn't answer, but shepherded her out of the room and along the corridor, supporting her when they started down the stairs and her legs threatened to crumple beneath her. It occurred to her that the soot-laden mist followed them everywhere, but she couldn't fathom what it was.

Cold air rushed in on her as they reached the outside of the building, and she stood still for a moment as the shock of it brought on yet another bout of coughing. Her lungs felt scratchy and raw, and when she tried to breathe it was a battle to get the air into her wheezy chest.

'What's going on?' she said in a cracked voice, puzzled by the buzz of activity and the sounds that filled the night air. The sky was black, sprinkled with stars, and the quadrangle was bright with the yellow lights of the buildings all around.

Someone pushed a wheelchair behind her, and the man who had brought her out here pressured her into it with his hand on her shoulder.

'Sit down and take it easy,' he said. 'You've inhaled a lot of smoke. Let the paramedics take care of you.'

He turned to another man and said, 'That's everyone accounted for. I've checked all the rooms and they're all clear.' The man he had spoken to nodded, and Amber realised that this other person was wearing a fireman's uniform. She looked around for a fire engine, and saw one in the distance.

Almost as soon as the two of them had finished speaking, a paramedic came and strapped an oxygen mask to her face. 'Breathe in as deeply as you can,' he said. 'The doctor will come and take a look at you.'

Someone—the doctor, she guessed—came over to her. She looked around for the man who had brought her here, but he had disappeared and she felt an odd, momentary sense of isolation sweep over her, as though she had been deserted. It was strange that she should feel such emptiness after the way she had resented his presence.

'I'll just listen to your chest,' the doctor said, taking out a stethoscope. He placed the end of the stethoscope on her back, over what she was wearing, and listened for a moment. 'I think we'll give you salbutamol to help with the bronchospasm,' he murmured. 'It will dilate the airways and help you to breathe more easily.'

Amber stared down at her thin nightshirt. Apart from a pair of briefs, it was all she was wearing. The shirt was made of brushed white cotton, with a delicate scattering of printed flowers across the scooped neckline and the hem. She didn't recognise it as belonging to her, but then through the fog that clouded her brain she remembered that someone had offered it to her last night. It didn't do much to cover her, and a large expanse of her legs was showing, much more than she would have liked.

The man who had brought her here was coming back to her now. His gaze moved over her and she was suddenly conscious of her state of undress and tried to pull the nightshirt a little further down over her thighs. Her hands were shaking, and the helplessness of her situation wafted over her like a draught of cold air.

She stared up at him in confusion. Her nerves must be more frayed than she'd realised. She wasn't usually this feeble.

'Are you all right?' he asked. 'Do you need anything?' His expression was restrained, serious even.

She said, 'No, I'm fine.' She thought about that, and then added, 'Actually, I have to go now. I have to go and check on my mother. I need to know that she's all right, and I have to go and find my clothes.'

'Is your mother in the building?' He looked concerned, all at once, his expression urgent.

She rubbed her forehead and tried to clear her thoughts. 'No. No, I...' She tried to make sense of everything. 'She hasn't been well lately. She's staying with my aunt.' She started to get up out of the wheelchair. 'I need to go and find my clothes and my bag.'

'I think they can wait.' He seemed to relax. 'If your mother's with your aunt, then there's no need to rush away, is there? It's very late, the early hours of the morning, and your mother is probably asleep. Your aunt will let you know if anything is wrong, won't she?'

Amber nodded, feeling a little foolish. Of course he was right. 'I'm sorry, I think I'm a little confused...disorientated.'

She began to shiver, and he said, 'That's only to be expected. It's probably a result of all the smoke you've inhaled.' He bent towards her. 'Let me put this around you. You must be in shock, and it will help you to feel better.' He wrapped a blanket around her, and gradually warmth seeped into her. 'Do you remember anything that happened?'

'Not really. I think I was asleep,' she said, slipping the oxygen mask off her face, 'and then you came and brought me here. I don't know what's going on. Is there a fire?' Her voice rasped at the back of her throat.

He nodded. 'It started in the kitchen of the building. Someone had left a pan of something on the hob and forgot to switch the heat off.' Reaching out to her, he put the mask back in place. 'Just try to keep breathing steadily.'

She held it away a little, so that she could speak. 'I wasn't in the kitchen. There was a party... someone's birthday. I don't remember an awful lot about it.'

'Perhaps you had too much to drink.' His expression was faintly cynical, and something in her instantly rebelled against being judged that way.

'You're assuming that,' she said stiffly. Who was he to criticise her? He didn't know anything about her.

'It was very difficult to wake you. You didn't seem to recognise the urgency of the situation.'

'Maybe, but it doesn't have to be because of alcohol.' It must have been the smoke that had done it, that had clouded her brain. She wasn't a drinker. She knew that much. Probably she'd had two or three glasses of wine at most.

Snatches of memory were coming back to her now, and she recalled that she hadn't known many of the people at the party. She had only been there because she was new—and for some reason it was important that she get to know them. She wondered why that should be.

The answer came to her in a flash of inspiration— a new job, that was it. She was about to start a new post and she was going to be working with them in A and E.

It began to worry her that some of her new colleagues-to-be might have suffered in the fire. 'Was anybody hurt?' she asked. 'Perhaps you should go and see to them. I'm all right. There's nothing wrong with me.'

His mouth made a straight line. 'One of the men, a doctor, has burns to his hands. Someone's jacket caught fire and he tried to put out the flames.'

'Oh, dear…that's terrible.' She looked up at him, anguish in her eyes. 'I'm so sorry.' A coughing spasm overtook her, and as soon as it was over she asked, 'Will he be all right?'

'I'm not sure yet.' He adjusted her mask once more, and she took a few moments to breathe in deeply. 'He's over there, being attended to by the doctor.'

Amber glanced to where he pointed, and saw the doctor applying something to the man's hands. She guessed that it was silver sulphadiazine cream and that as an added precaution the doctor would protect the patient's hands afterwards with polythene bags sealed at the wrists.

'Please, go and check on him, and the others. You don't need to stay with me. I'm fine.'

She took a moment to suck a desperate breath of air into her lungs. Across the paved courtyard, a sound alerted her, and she saw someone she recognized—a nurse who had introduced herself last night as Chloe. Chloe was standing with her little girl, a child of about four years old.

'The little girl isn't well,' Amber said now. 'I think she needs help.' Even through the noise of all the activity all around, she could hear the sound of the child's grating cough. She started to get up out of the wheelchair to go to her, but the man laid a hand on her shoulder and stopped her.

'Stay there. I'll go and see if she needs any help.'

He strode away, and Amber subsided back into her chair, breathing fast, wearily battling against the rawness of her chest. She guessed that he would go and alert the doctor or one of the paramedics if there was a problem. As for herself, she doubted she would be much help in the circumstances. Her lungs had been filled with smoke and she was suffering from the after-effects, battling to stay on top of things.

She watched him from a distance, and couldn't help noticing how very gentle he was with the child and her mother. He knelt down beside the little girl and put a hand on her back as though he would comfort her. A moment later, he was signalling for the paramedic.

Amber hoped that the little girl would be all right. She remembered seeing her last night, before her mother had put her to bed. She was an angelic-looking child, with hair that curled exuberantly and matched her mother's golden locks. She had Chloe's blue eyes, too.

The man gave Chloe a hug, and Amber wondered how well they knew each other. That wasn't the sort of hug that he would have given a total stranger. It was a familiar, easygoing hug that said he cared.

He waited while the paramedic attended to the little girl, and then turned and spoke to someone nearby. He said something to Chloe, and knelt down once more to talk to her small daughter.

Amber pulled off the oxygen mask. It was high time she took charge of herself. She couldn't sit out here all night. The doctor and the paramedics seemed to have everything under control here, but her own situation was fraught with difficulty. Her purse was in the building, along with her shoes and all her immediate possessions. How was she going to get herself home?

Perhaps she could call a taxi, if she could persuade someone to lend her the coins for the call, or maybe her aunt would accept reversed charges and make the call for her. Amber winced. It wouldn't be fair to wake her in the early hours of the morning, though, would it?

She stood up, and felt the cold paving slabs beneath her feet. Maybe one of the paramedics had a mobile phone on him and would let her make the call. She started to walk towards the ambulance, her gait a little unsteady but purposeful all the same.

'Where do you think you're going?' Her rescuer stood in front of her, blocking her path.

'I'm just going to make a phone call,' she said, gazing up at him in exasperation. Why did he always have to turn up at the wrong moment? She straightened up, drawing herself to her full height, which meant that the top of her head was just about level with his shoulders. What was he, six feet two?

She looked him in the eyes. She was doing her best to make a dignified exit, but as she tried to sidestep him, the blanket began to slip down from her shoulders, exposing a line of smooth, bare flesh, hampering her efforts and forcing her to make a strategic grab for the edges.

'Why do you need to make a phone call?' he asked.

Pulling the blanket around herself once more, she

tried to answer and found that she was struggling to get the words out. 'Why do you think?' she managed, between breaths. 'I need to go home.'

'Not just yet,' he said, leading her back to the wheelchair. 'You really should be going to the hospital. I would be grateful if you would just stay put for a little while longer. You're like a jack-in-the-box, and it's very wearing, trying to keep pace with you. First you resist my attempts to get you to move at all, and now it seems that you can't stay still for more than five minutes at a time. Please, do me a favour and sit down and try to relax.'

'I'm not going to hospital,' she mumbled.

Taking no notice of her mutiny, he manoeuvred her into the chair and leaned over her. Then he placed the oxygen mask over her face once more and she sent him a frustrated stare. She didn't see that she had much choice in the matter but to stay in the chair. She couldn't move if she wanted to. He was blocking her exit with every inch of his tautly muscled body.

She looked up at him, her eyes troubled. 'I should thank you for getting me out of the building,' she muttered, pushing the mask to one side. 'I didn't realise that you were trying to rescue me.'

'I guessed as much.' He smiled at her, a crooked half-smile that lit up his face and made her catch her breath all over again. She began to feel light-headed, weak in every limb, and she pulled in oxygen as though it was a lifesaver. He was incredibly good-looking, and those eyes—they meshed with hers and seemed to see right into her soul.

She looked away. Just thinking along those lines made her feel vulnerable. She said huskily, 'What were you doing there?' He wasn't wearing the uniform of a paramedic or a fireman, and she didn't recognise him from the party. In fact, he stood out from everyone here. He was dressed in an immaculately styled grey suit, and his shirt was pristine—or it would have been before he had battled the smoke.

'I'm here because my father owns this block of flats. He doesn't live locally and he asked me to come and check on things and report back to him. I expect he'll be along first thing in the morning to see what needs to be done.'

'Oh, I see. This must all be a dreadful shock to him.'

'It's more of a shock for the people involved, I imagine. We'll have to find alternative accommodation for them until the damage has been repaired.' He studied her for a moment. 'You're not one of the tenants, are you?'

Amber shook her head. 'It was late when the party finished, and I didn't want to drive home because I'd had a drink.' Her car keys were back in the flat. 'The girl giving the party said I could stay in her friend's flat. The friend is away just now, but she gave permission.'

He frowned, and she sent him an anxious look. 'It was all right to do that, wasn't it? I'm not getting her into trouble, am I?'

'No, that's all right. It's not your problem. I was just concerned because we didn't know that you were there until one of the other tenants remembered that you were in the room.'

Amber shuddered. 'So I could have still been in there now?'

'No. I made sure to check all the rooms, and the firemen were doing their own sweep of the building.'

She was humbled. 'Thank you for getting me out of there. I'm sorry I gave you so much trouble.' She gave him sideways glance. 'I owe you a lot, and I don't even know your name.'

'I'm Nick.' He looked at her thoughtfully. 'And you?'

'Amber.' She removed the mask and put it to one side. 'I'm fine now. I really must think about getting home. Why don't you go and look after the nurse and her little girl? I imagine they need you more than I do and I can manage perfectly well.' From the gentle, considerate way he had approached them earlier, she guessed that he knew them fairly well. Perhaps, as they were tenants of his father, he had become friendly with them.

His brows drew together. 'I doubt that. You seem to be in a worse condition than either of them. You were in the building for the longest time.'

He glanced over to where Chloe and her child were being treated by the paramedics. 'Chloe and Lucy will be all right. You don't need to worry. I've arranged for them to go and stay with Chloe's cousin until we can fix them up with something else. She's coming to fetch them.' He paused. 'In fact, I think I can see her arriving now.'

'That's good.' She tried a smile. 'Well, I'm sure there are other people who need help more than I do. Perhaps you should go and enquire after them…that poor doctor, for instance. I really need to start finding my way home.'

He gave her an odd look. 'The doctor's on his way to hospital, which is where you should be, too.'

She shook her head. 'I'm not going there.'

He studied her. 'All of the other tenants seem to be managing perfectly well. Most of them are fully dressed and aware of what's going on, and they seem to have managed to grab what belongings they needed before they made their escape. As for you, I really don't think you'll get very far in the state you're in.'

He made it sound as though she was hopelessly inadequate. 'You didn't give me a chance to get anything that I needed,' she said. 'I do seem to remember looking around for my shoes, and I'm sure if you had given me a moment I would have thought of other things I needed.'

'Best not to go there, I think,' he said. 'We both know that you were well out of it. I expect the fresh air has helped to revive you a little, but that's not saying that I would trust you to manage on your own.'

Clearly, he still thought that she was a party animal, but she didn't have the energy to argue the point with him. She glanced over at the building. 'They seem to have put the fire out,' she murmured. 'Do you think they would let me back in there?'

'Definitely not. It's probably not safe, and no one will be allowed in until the fire chief gives the say-so. That will probably not be for a day or two, given the damage.'

She made a face. 'All I actually need is a phone. Then I could arrange for a taxi to come and pick me up.'

'I'll take you where you need to go,' he said, and when she would have demurred, he added, 'That way

I can be sure that you will get there safely, and that you won't be wandering the streets in your bare feet. Are you staying at your aunt's house?'

'No, I have a place of my own.'

He looked surprised at that, and she wondered what he was thinking. Did he imagine that she was just a slip of a girl who was incapable of looking after herself?

He flicked a glance over her, and she realised that she must be in a totally dishevelled state. Her long chestnut hair was unruly at the best of times, and since she had unpinned it when she'd gone to bed last night it must be in full riotous disarray by now. No wonder he was looking at her as though she had lost her senses.

'I would appreciate a lift. Do you think we could go now?'

He nodded. 'Let me help you to my car. It's just around the corner from the building.'

He helped her to her feet, and said, 'Keep the blanket around you. I'll take it back to the paramedics tomorrow.'

His car was a top-of-the-range saloon, gleaming even in the darkness, and she guessed that even if he wasn't in partnership with his father, he must be doing well for himself. He helped her into the passenger seat and she sank back against the upholstery, her weary limbs thankful for the luxury and comfort that the interior offered.

He started the engine. 'Where do you live?'

She gave him the address with some hesitation. He was probably used to the best of everything, but her modest cottage was all she could afford, and at least it gave her the opportunity to be independent. She had come to Devon at her mother's request, but there was simply no room for her to lodge with her aunt.

'Are you going to be able to get in without your keys?' he asked as they drove out of the town and headed for the country lanes.

'I keep a spare, just in case. I've hidden it away.'

'You're not going to tell me that it's under a plant pot, are you?' He sent her an oblique glance.

She lowered her head and hoped that he couldn't see the flush of heat that ran along her cheeks. 'Not exactly. It's under a stone and there are several others around.'

'I might have guessed.' He raised his eyes heavenward and then concentrated on the road ahead.

He was a good driver, confident at the wheel, and he took the bends with ease. It didn't take long before they arrived at the house, and he parked the car by the pavement, coming around to help her out of her seat.

'This is it,' she said. 'It isn't much to look at, but it's just right for me.'

He was staring at the plain, stone-walled front, and she hoped that in the darkness he couldn't see the peeling paintwork at the windows. 'I'll just go around to the back and find the key,' she muttered.

He went with her, stooping to get the key when she located the rock in question. 'I'll come in with you and see that you get settled in all right,' he said, and she recognised a sinking feeling in her stomach. What was he going to make of her minuscule, dilapidated home?

At least the kitchen light was working. She flicked

it on and invited him inside. 'I'll see if I have any coffee in the cupboard,' she said. 'Would you like a drink?' It was the least she could offer after all he had done for her.

'Thank you. That would be good.' He was looking around, and she could see that he was finding the place hard to take in.

'I know that a lot needs to be done to make it right,' she said, as she stopped for a moment to wash her hands under the tap, 'but I bought it for a song, and I thought that in time I would be able to do it up. It needs some building work here and there, and I think there's going to have to be a lot of replastering, but it has great possibilities.'

He didn't appear to agree with her. He was frowning, and she thought it was perhaps a good job that he couldn't see the rest of the house. 'At least the cooker's working,' she said. She was rummaging in the cupboards, a struggle while she was holding onto the blanket in order to retain her dignity, but she had to turn around and say, 'Sorry, no coffee. Will tea do instead?'

'Tea will be fine.' He stared around him. 'You know you have damp in here, don't you?'

She nodded. 'It was one of the things that was pointed out in the survey, but I was assured that it could be put right. It's just going to take me a while, that's all.'

She made the tea and pushed the cup towards him. 'I'd offer you biscuits, but I'm afraid I haven't been able to get to the shops yet.'

'That's all right. I'd say biscuits were the least of your worries.' He looked at her as though he thought she must have been completely mad to take on a project like this. 'How on earth are you going to manage?'

'I'll get by,' she murmured. She took a sip of her tea to calm her nerves. What did he know of how the other half lived? From the looks of the expensively tailored suit he was wearing, and the car outside, he had never had to struggle for anything.

'Wasn't there any possibility of you going to live with your aunt—that is, assuming that her house is more habitable than this one?'

She grimaced. He wasn't one to mince his words, was he? 'She only has two small bedrooms, one for herself and my mother has the other one. We can't complain. We only moved to Devon a couple of weeks ago, and it was good of her to take my mother in.'

Her mother had been adamant that they should come here. There was every possibility that Amber's brother could be in the area, and she was desperate to get in touch with him.

She said cautiously, 'Your father must have been devastated by the news of the fire. Does he own other properties, or is the nurses' accommodation his only investment?'

'He has others, locally. Yes, it's a blow, but the insurance will cover the damage. The biggest problem is the disruption to the lives of the people who were living there.' He looked at her over his teacup. 'They were lucky to come out of this alive—you among them—and most of them will have lost belongings.'

'What happened to the man whose jacket was on fire?'

'He's OK. He escaped without any major injury. It's the doctor who saved him who has the problem.'

'How badly was he hurt? I know you said he had burns to his hands, but will he recover from them? Will he be able to work again?'

'From what I gather, he should come through this all right. It will take time for his hands to heal, though, and of course it will be some months before he'll be able to go back to work. It was a brave thing he did, saving his friend.'

'I didn't know him. I sort of remember seeing him at the party, but I wasn't sure whether he worked at the hospital—at the Castle Hill hospital.'

'Yes, he does—or, rather, he was about to start work as a senior house officer in the A and E department. That isn't going to happen now, of course. We'll have to find someone to take his place.'

Amber's eyes widened. He sounded as though he knew all about the A and E department. She said hesitantly, 'How is it that you know the ins and outs of it? Do you work there?'

He nodded. 'I'm the A and E consultant there.' He looked at her searchingly. 'You look taken aback. Is there a problem?'

'No...' It came out as a sort of squeak, and she tried again. 'No. There's no problem at all,' she managed weakly. 'I think I'm just overtired and things are all becoming a bit too much for me.'

She said it, but it was not the truth. The truth was she was shocked to the core to discover that he was in charge of the A and E unit. Her heart was thumping discordantly at the news, crashing about in her chest like a mad thing. Why did it have to be him, of all people? How on earth could this be happening to her?

'You're right, of course.' He pushed his cup to one side. 'Thank you for the tea. I should leave you to get to bed. Are you sure you can manage on your own now? Do you need any help?'

A bubble of hysteria welled up in her throat and she swallowed hard to suppress it. What was he suggesting…that he put her to bed? That would be one step too far as far as she was concerned.

'I can manage, thank you,' she said. 'Thank you for everything you've done for me. I do appreciate it.'

His grey eyes studied her. 'If you're sure?'

'I am.' A sudden thought occurred to her. 'Just give me a minute to find a robe, and I'll let you have the blanket back.' It came to her that she should have done that some time ago, but maybe she still wasn't thinking clearly.

She hurried up to the bedroom and put on a towelling robe. Seeing herself in the mirror for the first time in several hours, she was horrified at her reflection. Her hair was sticking out at all angles, a tousled mass of curls that had settled in chaotic disorder to frame her face and brush her shoulders, making her look like a wild thing. Added to that, there were faint streaks of soot on her forehead and along her cheekbones, and she guessed she must have run her hands along a soot-caked banister or a piece of furniture at some point. As for the nightshirt, it didn't bear thinking about. It revealed far too much of her slender curves.

Not wanting to see any more, she turned away from

the mirror and wrapped the robe firmly around herself. She hurried downstairs.

Nick was in the hallway, surveying the wrecked plasterwork with an expression of disbelief, but as she came down the stairs he turned towards her.

'Here's the blanket.' She handed it to him and then saw him to the door. 'Thanks again for all you've done.'

'You're welcome.' He glanced at her as he left, and she could see that he didn't quite know what to make of her. This man, of all men, thought she was a complete oddity, a partygoer, someone who was prone to taking leave of her senses, a crazy sort of woman who had bought a property that was falling down around her ears, and this was the man who was going to be her new boss in a couple of days' time. Could things possibly get any worse?

CHAPTER TWO

'CAN I get you anything, Mum?' Amber gave her mother an affectionate smile. 'Another cup of tea, or some more toast?' The kitchen table was littered with the remains of breakfast—cereal bowls and toast rack, along with two little pots of fruit preserves, but there was still some toast left and a portion of scrambled egg in a heated serving dish.

'Nothing, sweetheart. I'm full to the brim, thanks.' Her mother pushed her plate away and leaned back in her chair. 'Besides, you don't have to wait on me. It's enough that you managed to get here to share breakfast with us. You ought to be thinking about yourself. You start your new job today, don't you? And you must have an awful lot on your mind. Are you ready for it—do you have everything you need?'

Amber nodded. 'I think so. I sorted my medical bag out last night, and I put it in the car before I came here this morning. I just hope I haven't forgotten anything essential. I don't want to get off to a bad start.' Her stomach was churning at the thought of coming face to face with the consultant after all that had happened the other night, but she wasn't going to tell her mother that. It was probably better to leave her in ignorance.

'I'm sure you'll get on really well. You've been fine everywhere else you've worked, and they've been sorry to lose you, from what I heard.'

Amber's mouth twitched. 'Maybe. You always see the best side of everything—I think you might be just a little bit prejudiced.'

Her mother smiled and it lit up her face. 'I am where you're concerned. I just want you to be happy.'

'I will be,' Amber said, her voice taking on a serious note, 'just as long as you promise me that you'll make an appointment to see the doctor today.'

She studied her mother. She looked frail, and there were lines of tension on her face, giving her a drawn appearance. Her brown hair, which had once been vibrant, was now streaked with grey, and the sheen had gone from it. It feathered her cheeks but it did nothing to disguise the weariness of her features.

'Aunt Rose said that she would go with you,' Amber added. 'It's been worrying me that you're having so many bad headaches lately, and you know yourself that you need to get your health sorted out. You can't go on the way that you have been doing. The other day you were so giddy that you almost fell, and that can't be right.'

'You worry too much. I'll be right as rain. You just get yourself off to work and concentrate on what you have to do.'

Aunt Rose turned away from the sink where she had been refilling the kettle, and came over to the table. She began clearing away the breakfast crockery.

'You know what your mother is like,' she said, directing a stern glance towards Amber's mother. 'Julie's as stubborn as a mule when it comes to looking after herself. I'm just glad that she finally agreed to come and live with me, where I can keep an eye on her.'

'It's a relief to me, too,' Amber said.

Her mother gave them both a wry glance. 'I've managed well enough up to now,' she muttered. 'I don't know what all the fuss is about.' She pushed her chair back from the table and stood up slowly. Amber noticed that she steadied herself momentarily with a hand on the table's edge, but then she straightened up and walked towards the door that led into the hallway. 'I'm going to tidy my bedroom,' she said, 'but I'll be down to see you off to work, Amber. I think you can trust me to sort myself out.'

Amber watched her go from the room, and then sighed. 'I just know that she's going to try to wriggle out of it,' she said to Aunt Rose. 'If she doesn't see the doctor today, I'm going to ring and make an appointment for her myself. She's been worrying me more and more as the days go by.'

'I don't think the story in the newspaper helped very much,' Rose said. 'When she heard about the fire at the block of flats, and realised that you were there, she very nearly collapsed from the shock. I think she was terribly afraid that she might have lost you. She's never got over losing Kyle, and I think it would have definitely been the last straw for her if anything had happened to you.'

'She hasn't lost Kyle. He's still around, somewhere.' Amber frowned. 'I thought she was holding onto a last glimmer of hope—when your friend-of-a-friend said she'd heard that he might be down here, she insisted on coming to live in the area. It was perhaps just as well that we were thinking of moving anyway.' She paused, thinking it through. 'I suppose there could be some truth in it. After all, he loved this area when he was a child. Perhaps he wants to get back to his roots.'

'She's clutching at straws. The rumours could be way off beam, and I'd be surprised if he could remember having a home here at one time. It was a long, long time ago. But at least your mother has left notice of where she's living now—just in case he ever turns up at the old house. They're good people, the couple who moved into your old place. They promised that they would keep in touch, didn't they? And I have every faith in them. Though, if you ask me, it isn't very likely that he'll put in an appearance after all this time.'

'You could be right, but I hope for her sake that we find him. For years now she's been stressed out, worrying about where he is and what he's doing. I just hate to see her looking so ill.'

Aunt Rose made a face. 'You won't thank me for saying it, but it didn't do her a lot of good, living with your father. He was a difficult man at the best of times, and he caused her a lot of heartache. To be brutally honest, I wasn't sorry when the marriage broke up.'

Amber could understand how she felt. Any loyalty that she might have had to her father had disappeared long ago. He had been a strict disciplinarian, a domineering man, and she wasn't surprised that it had taken her mother so long to break free.

She glanced at her watch. 'I must go,' she said. 'I've a busy day ahead of me. Take care, Aunt Rose. Thanks for breakfast.'

Aunt Rose nodded, giving her a quick hug. 'I wanted to make sure that you had a good meal inside you before you went off on your first day in a new job. You'll do all right, I'm sure.'

She was a no-nonsense sort of woman, tall and strong, the opposite of her sister, and Amber hugged her in return and felt reassured that she could leave her mother in her care.

She collected her things together, said her good-byes and then headed towards town and the Castle Hill hospital.

She had been hoping that she might avoid bumping into the consultant as soon as she entered the A and E department, but it wasn't to be. She wasn't that lucky.

He was there, by the reception desk, talking to Chloe. He didn't seem to notice Amber as she walked in, and she kept a low profile, talking quietly to the desk clerk and generally gathering information about the set-up in the unit.

'I'll hand you over to Mandy, our triage nurse,' the desk clerk said. 'She'll give you a quick rundown of everything.'

'Thanks.'

Mandy had been at the party the other night, and Amber recalled that she was a lively girl, with dark hair that shone with good health and warm, brown eyes. She greeted Amber cheerfully. 'It's good to see you again. That was a terrible end to the evening, when the fire started, wasn't it?' she said. 'I'm just so relieved that we all managed to escape.'

'Me, too.'

'Come on. I'll show you where we keep every-thing. We'll start off round here at the back of the reception desk. That's where we keep most of the forms that you'll need.'

Amber followed her, and tried to keep track of where she would find blood-test forms, lab-request slips and relevant charts.

'I know it can be difficult when you start a new job, getting used to the place, but you'll soon get the hang of our system, I'm sure,' Mandy said.

'I hope so.' Mandy was friendly and helpful, and Amber did her best to concentrate on what the nurse was saying, but snatches of conversation came to her from the other side of the desk, and she couldn't help hearing all the ins and outs of Chloe's problems. She wasn't making any attempt to keep her voice down.

She was clearly was upset. 'Did you see this article?' she was saying. She waved a newspaper in front of Nick's face. 'It's all about the fire the other night, and they have a photograph of me on the front page— I can't believe they put my picture in the paper.' Her face crumpled. 'What am I going to do? If my ex-husband sees this, he'll know where I am, and he'll come after me.'

'That's not necessarily true,' Nick said softly. 'You're not living there now, are you?'

'No, but as soon as the repairs are done and I move back in, he's going to find me, isn't he?'

Nick gently placed his hands on her shoulders and made her look at him. 'You must stop upsetting yourself like this. I'll speak to my father, and between us we'll find you somewhere else to live. That will solve the problem, won't it?'

'I suppose so.' She stared up at him, her blue eyes wide and troubled. 'I'm sorry to lay this on you, Nick.

It's just that he frightens me so much. He was such
a violent man.'

'Try not to be afraid,' he murmured. 'If you're really worried, you should go to the police and get a
restraining order. In the meantime, can you stay with
your cousin until we get you fixed up somewhere?'

Chloe nodded. Her blonde curls shimmered in the
glow from the overhead light. She was a pretty girl,
and Amber could understand how any man would feel
protective towards her. She looked vulnerable and
needy, and the consultant was obviously responding
by giving her his full support.

Mandy was called away, and she left Amber to
familiarise herself with the system. 'I'll be back in a
while,' she promised. 'I just need to go and look in
on one of my patients.'

Amber nodded, and went on rummaging through
the various types of forms. After a while, though, her
mind began to wander.

Her mother had seen the same article in the newspaper, and it seemed that the fire at the accommodation block was the talk of the neighbourhood.

It just showed how great the power of the press
could be. What if she could use that power to her
own ends? Could it be one of the ways that she could
try to contact her brother? If he *was* living in the area,
it was possible that he would read the local news.

'What are you doing?'

She looked up with a start as a now-familiar male
voice intruded on her reverie. 'I'm sorry?' she floun-
dered, trying to get her wits together once more. She
gazed at her boss in confusion. 'Did you say something?'

Nick was staring at her with a look of exasperation that she was beginning to recognise.

'Yes, I did. I'm sorry if I'm interrupting your daydream, but I would appreciate it if you could drag your attention my way for a moment or two.'

She blinked. His sarcasm wasn't wasted on her. It seemed that she hadn't even managed to get through the first half an hour here without crossing him.

'I'm afraid I was a little preoccupied,' she mumbled.

He made a faint grimace. He said slowly, 'I was asking what you're doing behind the desk. It seems to me that you're in an area where you have no business to be. Is that correct?'

'Er, no…' She straightened up, a little intimidated by his brooding expression. 'What I mean to say is, it is all right for me to be here. I was just familiarising myself with the way things are organised. I'm going to be working in this department.'

He stared at her in disbelief, and then shook his head. 'No, I don't think you have that quite right.' He frowned. 'This is an A and E unit. Perhaps you were looking for the records office or something?'

Her mouth made an odd shape. 'Actually, I think you'll find that I'm your new senior house officer— or rather, one of them.'

He didn't say anything for quite some time, but simply studied her as though she had descended from another planet.

When the silence became unbearable, she thrust out her hand to him and said, 'I'm Amber Cavell…Dr Cavell. I don't think you were here when the interviews took place, but Professor McIntyre arranged everything in your absence. I'm here to start a staff grade posting.'

He stared at her hand, and when she started to think that he was going to ignore her, he finally grasped it and said in a kindly tone, 'You know, I'm sure there must have been some mistake.' He almost patted her hand. Then, collecting himself, he let her go as though he had been stung.

He said lightly, 'Even so, I must say I'm pleased to see you again and to find that you seem to have recovered from your ordeal.' He looked at her searchingly. 'I take it you have recovered?'

Amber disguised a wince. Did he think she'd taken leave of her senses once more? His manner was almost patronising. 'Yes, thank you,' she said. 'I seem to have come out of it with no after-effects. I'm very lucky, and I realise that I have you to thank for that.'

'Possibly.' He turned to the desk clerk, and said, 'Would you let me have the file on the new senior house officer post, please? There are a few details that I would like to check.'

It was Amber's turn to stare. Surely he wasn't going to search for a reason to have her evicted from her post before she had even started it? Could he do that?

The desk clerk hunted through a filing cabinet and handed him a folder. 'I believe this is the one,' he said.

'Thank you.' The consultant flicked through the paperwork, his dark brows edging closer together as the seconds passed. Amber watched him guardedly.

After a while, he looked up, and said in a clipped voice, 'Professor McIntyre's handwriting doesn't improve with time, unfortunately.' He looked at her once more. 'I was expecting a Dr Andy Carmel.' His mouth made a straight line. 'It looks as though I owe you an apology. I should welcome you to our department.'

He said it calmly enough, but his lips were stiff, and Amber wondered how much of an ordeal it was for him to accept her on his team. It didn't bode well for the future. Things were not going to be easy, working alongside him, that was for sure.

He said carefully, 'I'll get someone to show you around, and as soon as you feel ready, you can start seeing patients. Mandy will direct them your way.' He frowned as a siren sounded in the distance. 'You'll have to excuse me—we have patients from a road traffic accident coming in. You don't need to be involved with that—I already have the staff in place to attend to them.'

Amber had the feeling that he didn't trust her to assist, and already he was moving away, his mind seemingly elsewhere. Surely she would be able to prove herself to him over the next few hours and days?

She did as he had suggested, going on a quick tour of the department before she started work. She was worried about making a mistake—her nerves were already in shreds—but as the morning wore on, her professional instincts took over.

'There's a patient waiting for you in room three,' Mandy said at one point. 'Jack Carstairs. He's complaining of a sudden loss of vision, and the paramedic was querying migraine.'

'OK, I'll see to him.' Amber glanced at the chart

Mandy handed to her and then hurried towards the room.

Her patient was a man in his late fifties. 'Hello, Mr Carstairs,' she greeted him warmly, trying to put him at ease. It was clear that he was unsettled and anxious. 'I'm Dr Cavell, and I'm just going to have a quick look at you and see if we can find out what's causing the trouble. Can you describe the loss of vision to me?'

He answered her questions as best he could, and she made a quick examination, checking his perception of light and his ability to detect hand movement or count the fingers she held up before him. She became increasingly concerned as she went on to examine the affected eye through a slit lamp.

'There are one or two more things that I want to check, Mr Carstairs,' she said. 'I'd like to listen to your heart through my stethoscope to check for any murmurs and so on, and then I want to take some blood from your arm for testing.'

He let her proceed, and when she had finished and sent off the relevant samples to the laboratory, he asked worriedly, 'Do you know what's causing the problem?'

'I can't say for certain just yet,' she answered. 'It will depend on the results of all the tests. I've arranged for an ophthalmologist to come and take a look at you.'

'Am I going to lose my sight permanently?' It was a blunt question, and Amber thought he deserved an honest answer.

'I'm not sure,' she said. 'It's possible that you have a blockage in the retinal artery, and the outcome very much depends on how quickly we can move that blockage. We need to find out what's causing the obstruction in order to be able to treat it.'

'But you must have some idea?'

'It's probable that you suffered an embolism, and that might be because you have a degree of atherosclerosis. We won't know until the results come back. In the meantime, I'm going to attempt to lessen the pressure within the eye. That's probably the best way of trying to save your sight.'

He looked frightened, and she did her best to reassure him. 'I need to massage your eye,' she told him, 'because that may dislodge the embolus and allow the eye to recover a little.'

She settled him into a comfortable position and then for a few seconds she applied direct pressure to the globe. Then she released it and repeated the action several times.

There was still no sign of the specialist putting in an appearance, and Amber was beginning to be concerned. 'There is something else I can try, while we're waiting for the consultant,' she told the man. 'I can draw a little fluid from the eye to move the embolus even further away. It sounds horrible, I know, but don't worry—I'll give you a local anaesthetic. Try to relax and I'll do what I can to save your sight.' She called for assistance from a nurse, and Chloe came to help.

'Are you going to use the slit lamp?' Chloe asked, and Amber nodded. 'I'll need a tuberculin syringe and 27-gauge needle.'

Amber worked carefully for some time, and eventually she was relieved that the pressure within the eye had been reduced. She said, 'All right, Mr Carstairs...that's all finished now. Just rest for a while, and then I'll arrange for you to have a magnetic resonance angiogram so that we can see what's happened to the embolus now.'

He looked anxious and she said, 'It's nothing to worry about, I promise, and when we have a clear picture of what we are dealing with, we'll be able to give you further treatment to dissolve the blockage and to prevent any further damage. It all depends what the specialist decides once he's looked over your case notes.'

She smiled at him. 'You've been very brave. Take it easy now, and I'll leave you with the nurse for a while. I'm sure she'll answer any questions that you have.'

Chloe went to attend to him, and Amber hurried away to chase up the specialist.

'He's dealing with another emergency,' Mandy said. 'He said he would get down here as soon as he could.'

Amber wasn't happy about that. In cases like Jack Carstairs's, she knew that speedy treatment was imperative. A matter of a few hours could make all the difference. She had done what she could to save his sight, but it all depended whether he had been treated early enough.

She laid her stethoscope down on the desk, and began to write up her notes. Perhaps she should enquire into the possibility of Jack being treated with hyperbaric oxygen therapy. At least if she had set the wheels in motion, the treatment would be available if the specialist decided to go ahead. It was a fine line

to tread, but she went ahead anyway and organised it.

The last thing she needed was to be taken to task
by the ophthalmologist for not acting quickly enough
or for taking on too much and impinging on his area
of specialisation. She didn't know what the rules were
here, or anything about individual sensitivities, and
she didn't want to tread on any toes, but her patient's
welfare had to come first. If the consultant decided
not to go ahead with what she had arranged, nothing
had been lost.

She was just signing off on the chart when she felt
something tugging at her cotton over-shirt. Looking
down, she was startled to see four-year-old Lucy
standing by the desk.

'Do you know where my mummy is?' the little girl
asked.

Amber knelt down beside the child. 'Hello, Lucy.
What are you doing here? Is someone looking after
you?'

'Mrs Denney's looking after me. She's over there.'
Lucy pointed to where a woman was in conversation
with Mandy. 'I wasn't very well,' Lucy said, 'and she
brought me to see my mummy. Where is she? Do you
know?'

'Yes, she isn't far away. I'll go and find her and
tell her that you're here, shall I?'

'It's all right. Mandy said she would find her, but
she's talking to Mrs Denney. I want Mummy to come
and take me home.'

'She'll be here in a minute or so, I expect.' Amber

paused. 'You said you weren't feeling very well… what's the matter? Is there anything I can do to help?'

'My chest hurts. I want to go home.'

'Do you think you'll feel better there?'

Lucy nodded and Amber said cautiously, 'Does Mrs Denney look after you while your mummy's working?'

Lucy nodded again. 'She works in the nursery upstairs.'

'Oh, I see.' She looked at Lucy's pale face. 'I wonder why your chest's hurting. Did the smoke upset you the other day? I saw you coughing.'

'Yes, it did.' Lucy's chin jutted. 'It made me cough and cough and cough, and the man from the ambulance gave me some medicine. It still hurts, though.'

'Poor you. I expect your mummy will be here soon, and you can tell her all about it.' She got to her feet and put her hand out to the little girl. 'Shall we go and talk to Mrs Denney?'

Lucy went with her, and Mrs Denney put an arm around the child's shoulders. 'Your mummy's coming to see you, chick,' she said. She glanced around, and added, 'Here she is now, look. Why don't you go and give her a cuddle?'

The little girl ran off to her mother, and Mrs Denney said, 'Thanks for bringing her back to me. I was keeping a discreet eye on her, just in case.'

'Do you think Chloe will take her home?' Amber asked.

'I'm not sure. It may be that Lucy just wants a little bit of reassurance, and then she'll be fine. If that's the case, I expect they'll have a few minutes together and then I'll take her back up to the nursery. Chloe said it's all right to bring her down here if there's a problem. It's better than having the child upset.'

'It must have been a bit unsettling for her, having to move out of the flat,' Mandy put in. 'I expect she'll be fine in a little while.' She glanced at Amber. 'Do you want me to go and take over from Chloe?'

'That would be good, thank you. I have another patient waiting. Will you let me know when the specialist arrives?'

'Will do. Leave it with me.'

Amber went to tend to her next patient, a woman suffering from a fractured hand. It was a nasty injury, and Amber took her time checking that blood circulation had not been impeded.

When she had finished, she walked out of the treatment room and straight into her new boss.

'Sorry,' she said. 'I didn't see you there.'

'I gathered that,' he said dryly. 'It helps if you look around, you know.'

Amber winced. 'I was thinking about the patient I've just attended to. You're right, though. I'll look where I'm going next time.'

'You can come and examine the youth in room two,' he said, 'since you've finished in there. He's having some difficulty with his breathing. I'd be interested to see what you make of him.'

Amber followed him to the room. She guessed he was intent on watching her at work, as he was in between patients just now. She might have known he would check up on her.

Going into the room, she greeted the youth. 'Hello, Sam. I'm Dr Cavell. I understand you are having some problems with your breathing?'

The young man nodded, and she guessed from the way he spoke and outlined his symptoms that he was suffering from asthma. 'I'll just listen to your chest, if I may,' she said. Reaching into her pocket, she searched for her stethoscope. It wasn't there.

She looked around, a sense of impending doom settling on her.

'Is anything wrong?' Nick asked.

'Uh…no…that is, I seem to have put my stethoscope down somewhere.' She turned back to the youth. 'If you will just excuse me for a moment, I'll go and retrieve it. I'm fairly sure I know where I left it.'

The boy nodded, seeming unfazed by her lapse, but before she left him, Amber placed an oxygen mask over his face. 'Just breathe in as deeply as you can,' she said. 'I'll leave you with the nurse for a moment.'

She felt like a complete fool, and she daren't imagine what Nick was thinking. He didn't say anything aloud, but his expression said it all.

He followed her over to the desk, and watched her scan the surface. 'Is there a problem?' he said.

'Um…well, I know I put it down here,' she began, looking around, 'but it doesn't seem to be here any more.' She frowned. Where could it be?

'I'd advise you to keep your equipment close to you,' he said crisply. 'I wouldn't like to think of a patient expiring through lack of attention because you aren't able to examine him.' His eyes narrowed on her. 'Are you sure that you left it here?'

'Yes, I'm quite sure.' Her gaze ran over the desk and the assorted clutter. The stethoscope was nowhere to be seen. 'Perhaps,' she said weakly, 'I could borrow one?'

'Ask the desk clerk to issue you with one from supplies until you retrieve your own,' he said, his voice curt. 'But do try not to lose it, won't you?'

'I'll guard it with my life,' she said.

His brows drew together in a dark line. 'You know, Amber, I was brought in here by the management because they thought I could do something to improve the star rating of this department. Up to now, I consider that I have been doing a fairly good job. I would hate to think that all my work was going to be for nothing because you have joined my team. Bear in mind that we are already shorthanded because we have lost one of our senior house officers after the fire the other night, and I really need everyone to pull his or her weight.'

She stared at him, her expression stricken. 'I'll do my best, I promise,' she said feebly. From the way he was looking at her, she wouldn't be at all surprised if he wasn't thinking that she had been responsible for the fire in the first place.

'I really do hope that your best is good enough,' he murmured. He walked away from her and walked towards the treatment room they had just left. Halfway there, he turned, and said, 'Perhaps when you have found the equipment you need, you would do us the honour of joining us.'

Amber wished that the floor would swallow her up. He had sarcasm off to a fine art, didn't he? Wasn't she allowed to make any mistakes?

Mandy approached the desk. 'I've just had word that the ophthalmologist is on his way to see to your patient with the eye problem,' she said. She glanced at Amber. 'I couldn't help hearing some of what Nick was saying.' She made a faint grimace. 'You shouldn't take it to heart, you know. I think he's a bit under pressure just now, with Rob going off sick because of the burns, and now Chloe's asked if she could go home with her little girl. He's usually not too bad to work with.'

Amber made a face. 'I don't think I've made a very good impression,' she muttered. 'I don't know if he's going to take to having me around.'

A few minutes later, she picked up a chart and headed towards the treatment room where Jack Carstairs was waiting. With any luck, the specialist would be a bit more amenable than Nick Bradburn.

She wasn't very hopeful about her future working relationship with her new boss. He was cool and calm and in control, and he exuded authority from every pore, and that was all very well, but she had looked forward to working alongside someone with just a little more give and take.

Right now, it seemed that Nick was on his way to being a faint copy of her father, except that Nick had far more subtlety about him. He was an unknown quantity, but she hoped he would lighten up. She'd had her fill of overbearing, high-handed men.

She wasn't at all happy about what lay in store.

CHAPTER THREE

'HAVE you met the new senior house officer?' Mandy asked a few days later. 'I must say I didn't think we would have a replacement for Rob so soon. Nick did well to find him so quickly.'

Amber finished writing out her lab request forms and glanced up at the nurse. 'You mean Casey? Yes, I met him this morning as I was going for my break, and we shared a table in the cafeteria. He said that he was here as a locum until Rob was well enough to come back to work. I thought he was really nice.'

'I did, too. He wasn't too uppity to ask the nurses if he wasn't sure of anything, and I thought that was really good. Some doctors think it's beneath them to ask a nurse for advice.' She had been leaning on the reception desk, but now she straightened, saying quickly, 'Present company excepted, of course.'

Amber laughed. 'It's all right, I know what you meant.' She put her forms to one side and said, 'I wonder how it was that he was available at such short notice? Like you say, Nick was lucky to find anyone to fill in.'

'Casey said that he was in between jobs just now. He's just finished a stint working with the lifeboat rescue service, stationed just a few miles away from here along the coast, and he wanted a change. He said he was looking to specialise in emergency medicine, but by the time his contract had finished, all the posts had been taken. I think he was really glad to get this job.' Mandy paused, glancing at her. 'I'm surprised he didn't tell you that when you were in the cafeteria together.'

'Actually, we spent most of the time talking about how he covered for me this morning,' Amber confessed. 'I only just made it here on time, and I was praying that Nick hadn't seen me. I didn't want him to think that I was completely useless and that I wasn't ready to plunge straight into work.'

'What happened?'

'Some workmen turned up at my house to start renovating my kitchen. I wasn't expecting them until the end of the week, to be honest, but they had a slot and I didn't want to turn them away. By the time they'd finished asking me what was what, it meant that I was late leaving home. Then I had to drop the car off for its MOT test, and of course the traffic was bad this morning. I knew I had to get a move on to get here before Nick started wondering where I was.' She grimaced. 'I think Casey must have guessed that I wasn't quite on the ball and he kept Nick talking while I sorted myself out.'

'He's made a friend for life, then?' Mandy chuckled. 'You and he are bound to get on now, aren't you?'

'Too true. I need all the help I can get where Nick is concerned. I don't seem to be able to do anything right.'

'Talk of the devil...' Mandy said, her voice lowering. She flashed a quick glance over to the double doors opposite. 'Here he comes now. I'd better go and make myself look busy.'

It wasn't going to be difficult to do that, Amber thought. In this hectic A and E department there were very few moments when they could simply stop and chat for a while. At least now that Casey had come to work with them, the load should be a little easier.

'I see that you're managing to settle in and get to know everyone,' Nick remarked as he came over to her. He watched Mandy's retreating figure. 'There's a lot to cope with when you first start a new job, isn't there? And I guess it helps if you can make friends and ease your way in.'

'I suppose so.' She wasn't quite sure what to make of him. He sounded friendly enough, but he could just as easily be having a go at her for hanging around chatting. It was hard to tell with Nick whether he was being sardonic or just passing the time of day.

'Have you managed to locate your stethoscope yet?'

'Yes, thank you.' Her colour rose. 'It seems that one of the junior doctors picked it up and moved it out of the way. It must have been dislodged and landed in one of the wastepaper baskets. Luckily, someone spotted it and handed it back to me.'

'I'm glad to hear it. Don't forget to hand the replacement one back, will you?' His glance skimmed down her loose cotton top, and then he turned away from her, heading towards one of the treatment rooms.

She stared after him. How did he know that she still had it in her pocket? Was the man psychic? Of course, she had been meaning to take it back to the supplies room this morning. With everything that had gone on first thing, though, she hadn't got around to it yet.

This morning, when she had come in at a rush, she had hurried to go and look at the list of patients and find out who she was scheduled to treat first of all. She had decided to return the stethoscope to the supplies room later, and had pushed it down into her over-shirt pocket, out of the way. Her own stethoscope had been hanging around her neck. That was when Casey had stepped in and waylaid Nick.

Had Nick known all along what the subterfuge was all about? She pressed her lips together. It was more than likely. He probably didn't miss a thing.

At least the rest of the morning went by smoothly. She concentrated on treating each of her patients with professional courtesy and efficiency, and she was fairly pleased with herself for taking care of a good number of them.

Just as she was about to go off on her lunch-break, though, Mandy waved her over to the desk to take a phone call. 'It's a neighbour,' she said. 'I think there's a problem at home.'

Amber frowned and picked up the receiver. 'Mrs Tyler? Is something wrong?'

'I hate to disturb you at work,' Mrs Tyler said, 'but I went around to your house just a few minutes ago to drop off a parcel in the conservatory, and when I glanced through the window into the kitchen, I couldn't help noticing that water was flooding over the floor. The workmen went off for their lunch a few minutes ago, and I don't know when they are coming back. They said something about calling in on another job for an hour or so. I thought you should know what was happening.'

'Oh, dear. Thanks for telling me,' Amber said. 'I'll have to see if I can get away, otherwise it means calling up an emergency plumber, and I don't know how long they will take to arrive. I'd sooner be there to see what's going on.' She was trying to think quickly. 'Leave it with me, will you? Thanks again.'

She turned away from the desk. Why did this have to happen now, when she was at work and she didn't have access to her car? Frowning, she tried to decide what she should do. Perhaps she should be thankful that it was lunchtime and she was due for a break.

'You look worried,' Nick said, coming over to the desk and filing away a chart. 'Is it something to do with a patient?'

Amber shook her head. 'No, it's a problem at home…a flood, apparently. I need to go and sort it out, but I don't have my car—it's at the garage, having its annual service and MOT—and I can't guarantee that I will be back in time for the afternoon shift. I need to work out what to do. I could get a taxi, I suppose—that would be the quickest option.'

'But expensive, I imagine.' Nick glanced at her. 'I can give you a lift over there. I'm going on my lunch-break now.'

She stared at him. 'Are you sure? I don't like to take up your time. I'm sure you must have other ideas of how you want to spend your lunch-break.'

'Maybe so, but I need a full quota of staff here, and it seems the best solution right now for me to take you. Are you ready to go now?'

She nodded. 'Perhaps I should ring for a plumber to meet us there?'

He took her arm and ushered her towards the exit. 'I doubt you would find one who could come out at this short notice. From my experience, even emergency plumbers are in short supply. It helps if you have an insurance policy to cover eventualities, of course.' He looked at her questioningly, and she shook her head.

'It was one of the things I was going to get around to. I just haven't managed it yet.'

'I guessed as much. Perhaps we should see what the damage is and then you can decide what your options are.' By now they were outside the building, and heading towards the car park. Just a short time later, for the second time in a few days, Amber found herself sitting in the passenger seat of Nick's luxurious car.

'What work are you having done?' he asked.

'I asked them to start on the kitchen first. It seemed the logical place to begin, because at the moment it's the most important room in the house. I'm having the kitchen units replaced, and the builders are going to rip everything out, put in a damp course and a new floor, and then replaster the walls.'

'That sounds like a lot of disruption. How are you going to manage as far as meals are concerned in the meantime? Are you going to go to your aunt's house?'

'She's offered, and I will do occasionally, but I don't like to impose on her too much. I have a microwave and a toaster that I can plug in anywhere, so I'm not going to starve, and I can always get my main meals at the hospital. The cooker wasn't much good, anyway, to be honest. It came with the property and it needs to be replaced.'

It didn't take them long to arrive at the cottage, and Amber slid out of the car with a sense of trepidation. She wasn't at all sure what she was going to find, or how she was going to deal with it, and with Nick looking on she felt a little under pressure.

In the event, it was worse than she had imagined. The kitchen was a complete wreck, and water covered the floor. As she opened the door that led from the conservatory into the kitchen, the water flowed outside and into the garden.

'Well,' Nick commented dryly after he had looked around, 'they certainly managed to make a mess of this. Which building firm did you employ? Bodge-it & Sons?'

Amber couldn't speak for a moment. Her kitchen units hadn't been up to much, but now they were completely smashed, and broken pieces of wood littered the floor. It was just as though someone had taken a sledgehammer to them.

She said carefully, 'I thought they would unscrew them from the wall or something. I don't think I expected anything like this.' She was silent for a second or two, and then added, 'I suppose I'd better find the source of the leak. I've no idea where to begin, but from this devastation, I expect there's a damaged pipe somewhere.'

She looked over to where the sink unit had been, and then, gingerly, she started to make her way over there. If she removed some of the debris, she might have a clearer idea of what she was dealing with.

'Leave it,' Nick said. 'I'll see if I can find the stop tap. Do you have any idea where it might be?'

Amber thought for a moment. 'Actually, I think it's outside. I'll show you.'

They both went outside and located the tap. It was stiff with age and disuse, but Nick managed to wrench it closed, and then he went back into the kitchen and surveyed the damage once more.

'The water should stop flowing in a little while,' he said. 'Why don't you get a brush and help it on its way, while I see if I can find out where it was coming from?'

He seemed to know what he was doing, and she left him to it. After a minute or two, he said in a satisfied tone, 'Found it.'

She went over to look. He said thoughtfully, 'It looks as though your builders realised the pipe joint had broken down, and someone has tried to fix it with putty. It obviously didn't hold out for long.' His glance swept the kitchen, and then he said, 'It looks as though that's the tub they used, over there. Do you want to hand it to me and I'll put some more on?'

She did as he asked, and then ventured cautiously, 'Won't it break down again? I mean, it didn't last the first time, did it?'

'That's true, but I think I have some insulating tape in the boot of my car. I'll finish it off with that.'

She was glad that Nick had come with her. It didn't take him long to fix the problem, albeit temporarily, and her nervousness gradually began to dissipate.

'I can't thank you enough for what you've done. I'm not sure that I would have known where to begin.'

'The question is, what are you going to do about your builders?' Nick frowned. 'If this is a sample of their work, I wouldn't be very happy for them to proceed if this was my place. Are you under contract to them?'

'I didn't sign anything, if that's what you mean. We just agreed that they would start work and I would pay them more or less on a day-to-day basis—a sort of time and materials agreement.'

'I should think they owe you, after this morning's efforts.' He studied her. 'Are you going to let them carry on?'

She shook her head. 'No, but I'm not sure who I can get to replace them. When I was looking for a builder, I rang quite a number, hoping to get a quote for the work, but they were all busy. Then this man came along and knocked on my door, and said he was a builder and that he'd noticed I'd moved in recently and wondered if I needed any work done. I showed him around and he sounded quite knowledgeable, so I let him make a start.'

She hesitated for a moment, thinking things through. 'I can see that it was a bad move. To be fair to myself, though, I was reluctant to sign anything and commit myself, just in case anything went wrong.'

'That's something, anyway.' His expression was wry. 'It could have been worse, and you could have landed yourself with a huge catastrophe. If you like, I could have a word with my father on your behalf. Being a landlord, he needs to have a number of teams of workmen that he can trust to work on his properties. They're all tried and tested, and it may be that he can recommend someone to do the work for you. I'd suggest that you draw up a proper contract, though. I could get my father to look it over, to make sure that everything is as it should be.'

She nodded. 'I'm a little overwhelmed, just at the moment, but it does sound like a good idea. Could you give me a few days to think it over?'

'Of course. Take all the time you need.'

Amber looked around at the remains of what had once been her kitchen. A lump came up in her throat, and she tried to swallow, and fight back the tears that stung her eyes. It was such a silly thing to get emotional over. It was just bricks and mortar and a few kitchen units, but somehow it represented all her hopes and dreams. This was her first home, the first place that truly belonged to her, and she had such a vision of what it might be. Now all that was in ruins.

'Do you have a kettle amongst all this?' Nick asked.

She blinked and looked at him in surprise. 'Yes, somewhere.' She had to think for a moment. 'I think I moved it into the conservatory. I didn't have much time to clear everything out of the kitchen this morning, so I just dumped everything where there was a space.'

'I think I saw a chair in the conservatory,' he murmured. 'Perhaps you should come through and sit down for a while. It isn't too damp in there now, and you can get yourself together while I make us a cup of tea.'

He put an arm around her and gently led her away. At the back of her mind, she thought that perhaps time was getting on and she ought to be heading back to the hospital, but she was too shell-shocked to resist and, anyway, right then it seemed like a good idea. It was comforting to have his arm around her, and she was glad that he was there to take control.

Somehow, he managed to locate everything that he needed, and in a very short time he had made a pot of tea and they were sipping the hot liquid and looking out over her garden through the conservatory windows.

'The garden is going to be beautiful once the summer gets under way,' he said. 'It looks as though you have quite a few established flowering shrubs out there, and it probably won't take very much work to get it looking perfect.' He sat in a chair opposite her and looked into her eyes. 'Are you interested in gardening?'

She nodded. 'It's all a question of time, really. There are so many other things that need to be dealt with. I thought I'd chosen the best option, buying this place. I knew it was a mess, but I had this picture in my mind of how it could look someday.' She made a face. 'I'm not quite so sure how things will work out now. Nothing seems to be going quite the way I intended, at work or at home.'

As soon as she had said it, she began to regret her words. She hadn't meant to reveal to Nick quite how apprehensive she was of the way things were going at work.

He leaned closer, his grey-blue eyes compelling her to look at him. 'I wouldn't worry too much, if I were you. Things are hardly ever perfect, the way we want them to be, but I'm sure you'll get there in the end.'

He was being kind to her, and he reached out and

touched her hand as it lay in her lap. It was a gentle touch, and it meant nothing, she was sure, except to convey his sympathy, but she felt for all the world as though he had lit a spark within her and now her nervous system began to erupt in fiery response.

She said, as evenly as she could, 'You're being very understanding, but I'm not sure that I deserve all your sympathy. I'm still finding my feet at work, and things don't always go as well as I'd like them to.'

'I'd say that you were doing fine. You've only been with us for a few days, and already our ophthalmologist is singing your praises.'

Her eyes widened in surprise. 'Is he?'

'He told me that you had saved the sight of one of your patients. It was only by your quick thinking that the man had any chance at all of not being permanently blind in one eye. He said that you did everything possible for him, and that by the time he had been able to see to the patient he had feared the worst. Instead, he was very pleasantly surprised.'

Amber felt a glow of warmth inside. 'I'm glad that things worked out. I wasn't sure that they would.'

'You did well. You should build on that.' He looked at her thoughtfully, and then put his cup down on the table. 'We should start back to the hospital. Have you finished your tea? Are you ready to go now?'

'Yes, I'm ready.' She stood up and went with him, locking up and checking that all was secure before she went out to the car. 'I'll just run next door and have a word with Mrs Tyler before we leave, if that's all right.'

He nodded. 'That's fine.'

Amber told Mrs Tyler what they had done, adding, 'I'll give the builder a ring as soon as I get back to work. I'm not happy with what's happened here, and I'm going to tell them not to come back again. If they come back to you for the key, don't let them have it, and if there's any problem, give me a ring at work, would you?'

'I'll do that, love. I think you're very wise to finish with them, from the sound of things.'

Back at work, things were as hectic as usual. Chloe was working with Casey on a patient, but she took time out to have a word with Nick. She sounded upset, and Nick gave her his full attention.

Amber wondered at his patience. He had been so helpful and decisive in dealing with her predicament back at the cottage, and now he was giving Chloe his full support. He didn't appear to be at all fazed by having to sort out so many problems. At the same time, he managed to run the department with smooth efficiency, and she was full of admiration for his skills, both as a manager and as a doctor. She doubted that she would be able to cope with so many troublesome complications all at once.

'Lucy isn't very well again,' Chloe said, 'and I'm sure it has something to do with what happened last night. Any kind of trouble seems to aggravate her lung problems. It's as though her immune system goes on the defensive at the slightest hint of trouble.'

'What went on last night?' Nick asked. 'Is there a problem at your house?'

'I thought I heard a prowler. It was hard to see anything because of the darkness, but the neighbour's dog started barking, and when I looked out, I thought

I saw the shadow of someone moving about in the garden. I hope it isn't my ex. I don't know how he could have caught up with me.'

'Have you contacted the police? You need to let them know that you're concerned.'

'Not yet. I was afraid they would think that I was being a bit overwrought. It's been quite a while since we divorced, and he hasn't made contact with me. I'm just worried because we are trying to work out a settlement through the lawyers, and he's fighting me every step of the way.'

'I think you should talk to them and see if they can come up with a solution. At least if they're alerted to the fact that you're concerned, it might make them react more quickly should there be any trouble.'

Amber moved away and tried to get on with the job in hand. She had to try to put everything behind her and concentrate on her patients. Just then, Casey signalled that he needed a nurse to assist, and Chloe went back to him. Amber heard him say, 'Will you set up an infusion of lignocaine for me? I need to get this arrhythmia under control.'

Chloe set to work, while Casey attended to his patient, checking his blood pressure and his pulse.

Amber pulled out a chart and went to deal with a woman who was suffering an acute asthma attack. Some minutes later, she heard Casey call for help.

She glanced up at Mandy. 'Do you think you can carry on here?' she asked. 'I think we have everything under control now.'

Mandy nodded. 'You go. It sounds urgent.'

Amber hurried to Casey's side. His face had paled, and she saw straight away that he was worried.

'What's wrong?' she asked.

'My patient suddenly collapsed,' he muttered. 'I don't know how it came about. It shouldn't have happened, but his blood pressure has suddenly taken a dive, and he's starting to fit. I don't know what's going on.' As he spoke he was securing the patient's airway, intubating him and making sure that he received oxygen in high concentration.

'His circulation's failing,' Amber said. 'Let's get some fluids into him.' She worked swiftly, and added, 'Try giving him ephedrine, and let's deal with the fits quickly. Are you sure that he hasn't had an overdose of the lignocaine?'

'I don't see how that could have happened.' All the same, Casey went to check the infusion pump. He stared at her in bewilderment. 'You're right.' He turned to her, his expression filled with dismay. 'He must have received the wrong dosage. I just don't understand how it can have happened.'

Chloe said defensively, 'I didn't do anything wrong. I programmed the pump, but I'm sure I did it correctly. Casey checked it with me.'

Just then, the patient went into cardiac arrest, and Casey started chest compressions. Alerted to the danger, they all began working as a team to ensure the patient's survival.

Sometime later, Casey announced with some relief, 'I think we're over the worst. I think we have him back now.'

Amber nodded agreement. 'That was a close call.'

Nick came over to them, and she guessed that he wanted to know what was going on. She began to worry for Casey. He was new here and this hadn't been a good start. They still had no idea how the overdose had come about, but a mistake had been made somewhere along the line and things didn't look good for Casey, or for Chloe.

'Has there been some trouble?' Nick asked in a low voice, drawing them away from the bedside. He directed a nurse to observe the patient. 'I saw that you were worried about something that had gone wrong. What was the problem?'

'I think it was something to do with the infusion pump,' Casey said. 'I know that I worked out the correct dosage, but the patient appears to have received many times more than that. I'm not sure how it came about.'

'I know that I programmed it correctly,' Chloe put in. 'I hope nobody is accusing me of doing anything wrong.' She frowned at Casey.

'I didn't say that, did I?' Casey murmured. 'I just said that somehow the patient was given an overdose.'

'Is your patient all right now?' Nick asked.

'I believe so,' Casey said. 'I was treating him for ventricular arrhythmia, and I'm sure that I followed all the correct procedures.' He outlined what he had done.

Nick listened to him, and then said, 'There's always the possibility that the infusion pump malfunctioned. It doesn't happen very often, but on rare occasions there may be an electrical short circuit or a software problem. It needs to be investigated, at any rate.' He turned to Casey. 'Make sure that the pump is withdrawn from use right away, and report it to the bio-med engineering department. They need to check it out.'

'I'll do that,' Casey said.

A siren sounded in the distance, and the nurse who was on triage duty said, 'There's been a major incident—a pile-up on the motorway. The first casualties are on their way. We need to be prepared.'

Amber hurried to get ready for the incoming patients. She saw Casey speaking to Chloe, and guessed that he was talking to her about the infusion pump. He moved it to one side. Then Mandy called Casey to go and check on a man who had suffered a pneumothorax. The man was struggling for breath and needed immediate attention.

Amber spoke to the triage nurse, and while she was doing that, the lady from the nursery school approached the reception desk. Lucy was with her, and Amber could see that she didn't look at all well. She recalled that Chloe had been worried about her earlier, and she wondered what was wrong with the child. Surely, this couldn't still be the result of the smoke from the fire the other day? Did she have an ongoing illness? No wonder Chloe was upset. She must have a lot on her mind.

Chloe came hurrying to see her daughter, and the two of them went with the nursery school teacher to the doctors' lounge. After that, Amber had no time to dwell on what was happening.

'Here we go,' Nick said. 'They're bringing the first of the casualties in. I want you to work with me, Amber. Let's get started.'

The paramedics whisked a man and a woman through the doors of the A and E department, and

Amber went to check on the scale of their injuries. The man had multiple fractures and internal injuries and she could see why Nick wanted her to work alongside him. A colleague went to treat the woman.

Nick was cool and collected under pressure. He seemed to know exactly what to do, and his sure-fire touch over the next hour was what saved those poor people. Their injuries were life-threatening, but Nick acted swiftly, and between them he and Amber brought them back from the brink.

'Thanks, everyone,' Nick said when it was over. 'You all did very well.'

Amber was exhausted at the end of her shift. It had been an eventful day, one way and another, and she wasn't sorry to be going home. When she thought about what lay in store for her, though, her spirits sank. In the last few hours she had managed to forget all about the state of her kitchen.

She had no choice but to face up to it. Wearily, she went and fetched her coat from the doctors' lounge, and as she went towards the exit doors she caught sight of Nick walking alongside Chloe. They were ahead of her, and she saw that he was carrying Lucy in his arms, and the little girl was resting her head on his shoulder.

Amber watched them as they went to Chloe's car. They looked like the picture of a perfect family. He gently laid the little girl in her seat and strapped her safely in then went around to the driver's side to say something to Chloe.

Was he saying that he would see her at home? It looked that way. Nick's car was parked alongside Chloe's, and when the nurse reversed out of her parking space and drove out of the car park, Nick followed.

Amber felt as though she had received a blow to her chest. Was he going home with Chloe and her child? Everything in her cried out against that, and she couldn't understand why it should bother her so much. Why did that picture of them as a family come as such a shock to her, and why did it hurt so badly?

CHAPTER FOUR

'I'VE arranged for you to go and see the doctor today, Mum,' Amber said, as she cleared away the breakfast dishes. 'I don't want any arguments this time. You managed to wriggle out of the last appointment, but it's not going to happen again. You're not well and we need to find out what's wrong.'

'I really don't know why you're fussing so much,' her mother said. 'I just get a few headaches, that's all.' She sipped her tea, and looked at Amber over the rim of her cup. 'You're the one who needs to take care, living in that damp ruin of a place. I wish that you could have found somewhere different to stay. I'm sure you'll end up with a nasty chest infection.'

'I'm perfectly all right where I am. You're just trying to change the subject, and it won't work.' Amber finished stacking the dishwasher and gave her mother a stern look. 'We were talking about you, and your health. What is it that you're afraid of? Why are you so against going to see the doctor?'

Her mother lowered her head and didn't say anything, but Aunt Rose answered for her. Putting aside the morning newspaper that she'd been reading, she said, 'I'll tell you what it is. She thinks that the doctor is going to find something terribly wrong with her, and she'd really rather not know if it's anything bad.'

Amber's expression softened. 'Oh, Mum, I don't think that there's anything dreadful going on. I just

65

think that you need to have your blood pressure checked, that's all. It's far too high, and you need treatment for it. The doctor will probably just pre-scribe some tablets to bring it down. I'm sure there's nothing for you to worry about.'

Her mother's glance flicked over her as though she was trying to work out whether Amber was telling the truth. 'You think that's all?'

'I do.' She went over to where her mother sat at the table, and stroked her hand. 'I wish you had told me before what was on your mind. I could have re-assured you.' She searched her mother's face. 'Is this why you were so anxious to find Kyle—did you think that something bad was going to happen?'

Her mother made a face. 'I think that was partly it,' she confessed. She slumped a little, looking as though all the steam had escaped from her, as though she was exhausted. 'I've been feeling quite wretched these last few weeks, to be honest, and I was afraid that I wouldn't see him again before...well, you know.'

She hesitated, and then went on haltingly, 'It's been so long since I saw him, or heard from him, and I miss him so much. I wish that I knew what was hap-pening to him, and what he's doing with his life. I just want to see him again.'

Amber felt her mother's sadness as though it was her own. 'You know, I thought I might put an advert in the local newspaper to see if we can find him. Nothing else that we've tried seems to have worked, but someone might see that and it could trigger off a memory of some sort. We might at least find out something of his whereabouts. It's worth a try, don't you think?'

Her mother's face lit up. 'Yes, I think it's worth a try. Would you do that for me?'

'I'll do it for both of us,' Amber said. 'He's my brother, remember. Well, my half-brother, but I haven't seen him since he was a young lad, and I'd like to feel that he was coming home at long last. I want my family back, too, you know.' She smiled at her mother. 'Tell you what, we'll make a deal—you go and see the doctor, today, and then I'll go to the newspaper office.'

'All right. I'll do it.'

Amber and Aunt Rose gave a joint sigh of relief. 'Thank heaven for that,' Aunt Rose said. 'I was beginning to think we'd never get that settled.'

Amber went to work feeling much easier in her mind than she had for a long time. Aunt Rose would make sure that her mother went to the doctor's surgery, and at least she herself could rest easy now, knowing that they had set things in motion.

She arrived at the A and E department in good time, and was surprised to see little Lucy sitting in the doctors' lounge. She was at a table, busily colouring in a picture from a book.

'Hello, chick. It's nice to see you again. Are you waiting for your mummy?'

Lucy looked up. 'Mummy's working. She said she's coming in a minute.' She went back to her colouring, and Amber went to stand by her and look at what she was doing.

'That's a lovely picture,' she said. 'Do you like colouring?'

Lucy nodded. 'I bringed my book with me 'cause we have to wait to see the doctor.' She screwed up her nose. 'I don't like seeing the doctor.'

'Oh, dear. That's a shame.' Amber was a bit at a loss. 'I'm sure the doctor is very nice. Usually doctors want to make you feel better when you're poorly.' Amber had no idea why Lucy would be waiting to see the doctor, unless it was something to do with the smoke she had inhaled the other day. It seemed odd that the child was sitting here all alone, too.

Amber looked around, and just then Casey appeared from the alcove where the coffee-machine stood. 'Hi, Amber.'

'Hi.' She smiled a greeting, but her mind was elsewhere and she turned her gaze towards the child. She was still concerned about what the little girl was doing here.

Casey must have seen her puzzled expression, because he said, 'It's all right. She's not on her own. I said I would look after her while I was on my break. I was just making coffee. Can I get one for you, too?'

Amber glanced at her watch. 'I'd like that,' she said. 'I've just about time to drink it before I start my shift. I don't want Nick having a go at me for being late. I'm doing my best to keep on the right side of him. I've been making the odd mistake with one thing and another, here and there, and I don't want him to think I'm totally inept.'

'You're all right. He's only just arrived himself. He came in with Chloe, and I think he's gone to his office to clear up some paperwork before he makes a start.' He glanced at her thoughtfully. 'I think you're a good doctor. He'd have to be blind not to see that.'

She made a faint smile. 'Thanks,' she murmured. 'You're very kind. It's a pity you're not the one in charge.' She sent him a swift glance. 'Are you settling in all right?'

'I think so. I could have done without yesterday's crisis with the overdose, but at least Nick gave me the benefit of the doubt. I know I didn't miscalculate. I just can't think what happened.'

'Perhaps Nick was right, and it was a faulty infusion pump.'

'Maybe.'

He dipped back into the alcove. A moment later he handed her a mug of coffee, and then went and sat down beside Lucy. 'You're doing very well,' he said to her. 'I wish I could colour as well as that.'

Lucy gave him an old-fashioned look. 'You have to practise,' she said. 'I can do it because Nick showed me how to keep the colour inside the lines. He showed me last night.'

Amber watched the child as she bent to her colouring once more. The girl's innocent words troubled her. Had Nick stayed with Chloe for the whole night? They had left here together yesterday, and according to Casey they had arrived here together this morning, so it certainly seemed as though he had been with her for all that time.

Of course, he had every right to do as he pleased, and there was no earthly reason why it should bother her. Even so, the thought made her feel strangely unsettled, totally at odds with herself.

Just then Chloe came into the room. 'Sorry for leaving you for so long,' she said, coming over to the table and giving her daughter a hug. She gave Amber and Casey a quick smile.

Turning to Casey, she said, 'Thanks for watching over her for me. It's all been a bit of a rush for me this morning, and now we have to go over to the respiratory unit for her check-up.'

'Is something wrong with her?' Amber was troubled. It must be very distressing to have a child who was ill. Chloe was a single parent, and she had a difficult job to do. This must be an added worry.

'She had pneumonia a year ago, and it's left her with a few problems. We have to keep an eye on her chest to make sure that everything is all right.'

'I don't suppose the smoke from the fire did her much good,' Amber said with a frown. 'Have there been any lasting effects?'

'She was poorly for a while,' Chloe said, 'but the doctor put her on a nebuliser, and I think she'll be all right. We have to be so careful.'

'I'm sorry. That must be hard for you.'

'It's certainly not easy, but we get by. It helps that Nick has been really supportive. I haven't had to worry about asking for time off, and he's been really helpful. What with the fire, and the prowler, everything has been getting me down just lately, and now it turns out that there was a robbery in our area last night. It's very upsetting.'

'You mean there was a robbery near to where you live?' Amber said.

'That's right. I heard the police cars in the early hours of the morning, and then I heard all about it this morning. Nick says there are some wealthy properties close by where I'm living, and one of those was targeted. I don't think they would pick on me—I've nothing worth stealing—but it's disturbing, all the same.'

She turned to Casey. 'Thanks again for watching over her.' Holding out her hand to Lucy, she said, 'Come on, Lucy, it's time for us to go now.'

Lucy gathered up her book and pencils and left the room with her mother. 'Bye,' she said.

'Bye. Take care.' Amber finished her coffee and then went to wash out her mug at the sink. 'I need to get to work,' she told Casey.

'Me, too. I'll come with you.'

Amber tried to put thoughts of Nick and Chloe out of her mind as she dealt with her patients, and soon she lost herself in the adrenaline rush of tending to the wide variety of casualties that was brought in.

She didn't see much of Nick until later on in the morning, but he approached her as she was suturing a man's head wound. Her patient had a nasty gash across his temple, and she was doing her best to make a neat job of bringing the edges of the wound together.

'Did you have a word with your builder?' Nick asked. He nodded to the patient, and came and leaned against the edge of the table so that she was inordinately conscious of him. His long legs were stretched out, one foot crossed over the other at the ankle. He was wearing dark trousers and a crisp shirt, and his tie was a subtle shade of blue and grey, blending in a satisfying way with the darker blue of his shirt.

She made an effort to concentrate on her work. 'I did.' She grimaced. 'It wasn't a very pleasant experience, but I managed to sort it out in the end. He won't be coming back.'

'I think you've made a wise decision. Have you made up your mind about what you want to do? Would you like me to ask my father to find someone?'

Amber finished the suturing and handed her patient over to a nurse who would dress the wound.

She turned to Nick, and together they walked away from the treatment room. 'I think that would be a good idea, but it all depends on what they want to charge for doing the work. I know that building costs can get out of hand and I have to be careful about what I can spend.'

'I understand that. I'll get in touch with my father and see what he can come up with.'

Casey was working close by, and now he glanced their way. 'What's this about building work?' he said, looking at Amber.

'I've bought a run-down cottage—I bought it cheaply, and thought it would be a good idea to do it up. It's just that I'm discovering there's a lot more work to be done than I realised. I'm desperately hoping that I've not bitten off more than I can chew.'

'It sounds like an interesting project, at any rate. I'd quite like to see what you've taken on...if you don't mind visitors, that is?'

Amber gave a wry smile. 'You might not be so keen when you actually see it, but you can come along, by all means. I'd be glad of any input. You might have some better ideas than I do about the best way to tackle it.'

Casey's mouth made a curve. 'That's settled, then.

I might be able to help. I've had a little bit of experience with old properties. I've lived in a few.'

Nick glanced from one to the other of them. 'Mandy tells me there are patients coming in on a blue light. We should get ready for them.'

His expression was austere, and Amber wondered what had happened to change his mood. Did he think that they were lax, taking time out to chat? And yet hadn't he started it? Perhaps he was just going into professional mode now that he knew patients were on their way.

It bothered her that she constantly felt that she was out of sync, that she was failing in some way. Perhaps it was just that she was new in this job, and oversensitive, but Nick's mouth was set in a hard line and that made her uneasy.

When she had finished work for the day, she called in at Aunt Rose's house. 'How did it go at the doctor's, Mum?' she asked, dropping her bag down on the hall table and going into the living room. Her mother was sitting in the easy chair, reading a book and frowning as though it hurt her eyes, but now she put the book to one side and looked up at her.

'It went all right, I think, but I have to go and see someone at the hospital,' she said. 'The doctor said she wanted to check things out before she wrote out a prescription.'

'Your mother's records showed that she has had high blood pressure before this. They're going to fit her up with a recording device and monitor her over a twenty-four-hour period,' Aunt Rose said. 'Unfortunately, we have to wait a while for the appointment to come through.'

'At least we've made a start,' Amber murmured. 'I'm going to pop into the newspaper offices at lunchtime tomorrow and set things in motion there, too.'

'That's good,' her mother said with satisfaction. 'Now, come and tell us about your day. Did everything go all right? You haven't crossed swords with that boss of yours again, have you?'

'Not today.' Amber told her about Nick's suggestion that his father would help find a builder for her. 'I just hope things work out better this time. I really want to get on with renovating the cottage.'

'My thoughts exactly,' her mother agreed. 'I hate to think of you living in that place.'

Amber wasn't thrilled about it either, the way things were at the moment, but she set her sights on having everything put right.

As things turned out, Nick's father came to the cottage just a few days later, as they had arranged. Amber opened her door to him in the afternoon, and greeted him warmly.

'Mr Bradburn, it's good to see you. I wasn't sure whether you would manage to fit me into your schedule,' she said. 'I know that you're a busy man.'

'Call me James. Let's not be formal,' he said with a smile. 'Nick told me that this was your afternoon off. I didn't want to mess you about.' He was a tall man with dark hair showing streaks of grey at the temple, and Amber reflected that she could see his son in him. She pulled the door open wider and ushered him inside.

'Come through, and I'll show you around.'

'Thanks. I brought Nick with me, and the builder, Tony Macclesfield. I hope you don't mind? I thought it would be easier to get it all sorted in the one afternoon.'

Her eyes widened. Nick was with him? She glanced outside, and saw Nick's car pull up behind his father's. There was another man sitting in Nick's car, and she guessed that he was the builder.

'They came together,' Nick's father explained, seeing her confused expression. 'Tony lives nearer to Nick than he does to me.'

'That seems logical, then,' she murmured. She watched Nick get out of the car, and already her heart was thumping. He was dressed in casual clothes, dark-coloured trousers and a blue linen shirt that looked good against the faint bronze of his skin. She was so used to seeing him in A and E, smart, mostly wearing well-cut suits that looked impressive on his well-proportioned frame, but he looked equally eye-catching right now.

She said hello to Nick and the builder and then ushered the men along the hallway.

'I hope you didn't mind me coming along?' Nick said. 'I thought it would be simpler if I knew what was going on, and then I can liaise between you and my father and Tony if necessary.'

'That's fine. It's probably a good idea.' Her voice sounded a little hoarse to her ears. Nick's tall frame brushed hers momentarily as he moved along the corridor, and her nervous system immediately went on red alert.

She wished that he didn't have this effect on her. How was she supposed to think clearly when her pulse was racing and the blood was thundering through her body? And why was this happening to her, anyway? She wasn't involved with him, other than at work, and there was no possibility of that changing, was there? She had always been cautious, and at the back of her mind she worried about getting deeply enmeshed with anyone. Her mother's experiences had been enough to put her off.

'Perhaps you would like to show us around?' James Bradburn said, a dark brow lifting in enquiry.

'Yes, of course. It's difficult to know where to start, but perhaps I'll show you the kitchen first—or, rather, what was the kitchen.'

She led the way, explaining what she had hoped for in the kitchen, and then she showed them what could possibly be a utility room. At the moment, it was just bare walls with plaster missing in part and brickwork showing through in other places. 'I thought this would be a good place to put the washing machine and tumble drier. It isn't very big, but it would be really useful and save space in the kitchen.'

The other rooms were equally neglected. The builder made notes as they progressed through the house, and James said, 'Do you not have anyone who could help you out with all this? It seems a lot for a young woman to take on. Do you have any family who could advise you? Your father, perhaps?'

'There's no one, really. I haven't seen my father for some years now.'

'Oh? I'm sorry to hear that.'

'You needn't be. We didn't get on very well. To be honest, it was a relief when he left us—my mother and me.'

He sent her a thoughtful glance. 'Are you sure that your mother felt the same way?' He hesitated, and then added, 'Forgive me. That was blunt. I'm used to speaking my mind, and of course I realise that it's none of my business.'

'It's all right. I don't mind.' She saw Nick's glance flicker over her. 'My mother asked him to leave. It had never really been a happy marriage, and I think she had gone along with his overbearing ways for such a long time that she had to pluck up courage to do it, but in the end she made it clear that the marriage was over. In a way, I admire her for standing up to him after all that time.'

'And now you're happy to stand on your own two feet, I imagine. Well, that's good.' He looked around. They were standing in what should have been the guest bedroom, and he said, 'What plans did you have for this room?'

'I think I'm more concerned about what needs to be done structurally. Perhaps if you and Tony could let me know what basic work has to be done, I could decide what extras, if any, I can afford.'

'That sounds fair enough. Shall I talk it through with Tony, and we'll make a list? We'll perhaps need to go back through the house again, just to be certain. I think he'll want to look in the attic as well, and then check your roof.'

Amber nodded. 'I'll go and put the kettle on, and when you're ready, we can sit down and have a cup of tea.'

She went downstairs to the kitchen, and was surprised when Nick followed her.

'I think they'll get on better without me being there for the moment,' he said. 'I'll give you a hand with the tea.' He looked around, and added, 'At least you

still have an electricity socket in here. I see that
you've brought in a table from one of the other
rooms.'

'I thought it would make things easier. I had a
plumber come and get the water back on, so that at
least I can do the basics in here.'

She set out cups on a tray, and Nick went to search
for milk and sugar. He said, 'I couldn't help hearing
what you said about your father. It's unusual, surely,
for families to drift so far apart? It can't have been
easy. How did it affect you? What went wrong?'

'I think he wanted a son, not a daughter. He didn't
really take much notice of me. Perhaps I was just a
small child who disappointed him and got in the way.
My mother already had a boy from her first marriage,
my half-brother, but Kyle was six or seven years old
when they married, and my father never took to him.
I'm not sure why that was. Perhaps it was simply that
he wasn't his own flesh and blood, but as time went
by Kyle could never live up to his expectations. My
father was a police officer, a very stern disciplinarian.
I was very young, but even so I noticed that there
wasn't much love between them.'

'It's a sad story.' Nick frowned. 'So, what happened with your brother? I don't think I've heard you
mention him before this. Did he manage to work
things out?'

'No, he never did. He was in trouble a lot, at school
and at home. The police were often around, and it
upset my mother and made my father angry. I wonder
if it was inevitable, really. Kyle had lost his own father when he was very young. He died, and I suppose
that must have had a terrible effect on a little boy.

Then when his mother—my mother—married again, his world changed, and not for the better. Things went from bad to worse.'

'So where is he now?'

'I don't know. He left home when he was sixteen years old, and I think he joined the army. He had to have permission, of course, because he was so young, but he started off in the territorial branch, and then I heard that he signed up for a longer term. After that, I heard that he had been posted abroad. We had letters and cards for a time, but he wouldn't come back because of his stepfather.'

She stared absently into space for a while. 'I think that's what finally gave my mother the courage to divorce my dad. She couldn't bear losing her son.'

'I'm so sorry. That must have been difficult for you, too, losing your brother.' Nick ran a hand gently along her arm, and she suddenly realised that he had moved closer to her, so close that she could feel the warmth of his body against hers. His touch was soothing, a caressing gesture almost, and it comforted her. He was right in what he said, because in a way she was grieving for her brother. She had been very young when he had left home, but she remembered getting on well with him, and it was as though part of her was missing.

'I shouldn't have burdened you with all this,' she said, 'but you're a good listener. I think it helped to be able to talk about it.' It was true. Nick was being sympathetic towards her, and kind, and it felt good to have him near.

'I'm glad that you told me. I've been so used to having a good relationship with my parents, it's hard to imagine how it can be for some people.' He gave a faint smile. 'You've done well to rise above it. I don't suppose it was easy for your mother to put you through medical school, but here you are, a fully qualified doctor.'

'It was something I always wanted to do. A friend of mine was ill for a long time, and I suppose that's what made me think of going into medicine in the first place. My friend is well now, and that's all thanks to medical science. As for my mother, I think she wanted to make sure that at least one of her children had the best out of life, so she did everything that she could to help me.'

Nick's father came into the room just then with the builder, and Nick moved away from her a little.

'I think we've looked at everything we need to,' Tony said. 'I can probably tell you the good news along with the bad news, if you're ready for it?'

Amber made a wry face. 'I'll go and find some more chairs. Then we can all sit down and you can let me know the worst.'

They talked for some time, and at the end of it Amber knew that, as well as having the damp course put in and the majority of the rooms replastered, the electrical wiring needed to be renewed. The roof, thankfully, was in fairly good condition, apart from a few tiles that needed to be replaced.

'I can get an electrician to come in and sort the wiring out for you,' Tony said. 'What you need to do is let him know where you want all your sockets. If you get those positioned correctly, it will save you changing things later, when you come to put kitchen units in and so on.'

'OK. I'll sort that out, and you can make a start as soon as you're ready. I won't make any decisions about actually having the kitchen units fitted until I know what I can afford, and the same goes for the built-in units in the bedrooms. You can go ahead with the basic work, though.'

It had been a productive afternoon, and after they had left, Amber wandered around the house and wondered what it would look like when it was finished. It was good of Nick to get his father involved on her behalf. She could just about afford what was being planned, and everything else could wait for a while.

At work next day she stood alongside Casey and helped him with a patient who had collapsed in the waiting room. The man was in his early thirties, and together they secured his airway and his vital functions.

'He hadn't got as far as being checked by the triage nurse,' Casey said. 'I've checked him for signs of injury, but apart from the bang to his head when he fell, there's no suggestion of trauma that would have caused him to collapse.'

'What about an existing condition, or an overdose?' Amber asked.

Casey shook his head. 'I've looked through his pockets and so on for tablets or cards, but there's nothing to warn me about anything of that sort.'

'Do we have any of his medical history on the computer?'

'No, Mandy's checked. It looks as though he's moved here from another area, and we don't have any information on him yet. Mandy's going to follow it up.'

'He's very pale, and his heart rate is very fast. I'll do a blood glucose and get a full blood count. He could be anaemic.' She looked at the man once more. He was about the age that her brother would be, and he had just moved to the area, too. They knew nothing at all about him, and for all she knew he could be alone in the world. It was so sad how things turned out sometimes.

Casey nodded. 'He's thin, too. I wonder if he's been losing weight.' He was examining the patient's hands, and he said suddenly, 'Look at this. Look at the pigmentation in the palmar creases. You know, we could be dealing with Addison's disease.'

'That's true, but if that's the case, why wasn't he carrying a steroid card?'

'It could be that he hasn't been receiving any treatment, or that he's decided not to take the tablets for some reason.' Casey was frowning. 'I think we should take blood for cortisol and ACTH. I'm going to start volume replacement with plasma expander, and if he is having an Addisonian crisis, I want to start treating him as soon as possible—maybe before the tests come back.'

'I agree. What did you have in mind?'

'Hydrocortisone sodium succinate IV.'

'I'm wondering if he has an infection of some sort.' Amber was listening to the man's chest through her stethoscope, but now she looked up. 'That could have precipitated the incident.'

'You're right. We'd better give him antibiotic cover as well.'

It was some time later that their patient began to show signs of recovery. Casey gently questioned him, and the man said, 'I'm sorry to have caused such a fuss. I forgot my tablets. I only moved here last week, and I meant to go and get a prescription, but I had to sign on with a new doctor and it was all a bit of a hassle. I'm sorry for putting everyone to so much trouble.'

'That's all right. We're just glad that you're out of danger now. You must remember to carry your steroid card with you at all times. It's very important.'

'I will.'

Amber went and spoke quietly to the man. 'You must try to take care of yourself,' she said. 'You're young, and you don't want to end up back in here, do you?'

'That's true, but you've been very kind.' The man gave her a wry smile, and Amber gave his shoulder a light squeeze.

She moved away from the bedside and went over to the desk. A few minutes later, Casey joined her there.

'That turned out better than I expected,' he said. 'Thanks for your help.'

'It was a bit worrying for a while, wasn't it?' Amber agreed.

'It seems to me things are often like that around here.' He smiled at her. 'How did you get on yesterday? It was your afternoon off, wasn't it? Did your builder turn up?'

Amber nodded. 'He's going to sort things out for me. My only problem is what to do about the kitchen. I can't really afford to have someone fit it for me, so

I'm going to have to buy the units and fit them myself. It can't be too difficult, can it?'

'I could help out with that,' Casey offered.

She looked at him doubtfully. 'I don't know…it's a lot to ask.'

'I don't see it that way. I could fit your units, and you could feed me in return. I hate cooking, and that way we both get a good deal, don't you think?'

She smiled at him. 'I think that's an offer I can't refuse. I just hope that you haven't bitten off more than you can chew. It might take longer than you expect.'

Casey shrugged, his mouth making a crooked line. 'Then I guess I get to have more meals, and that's probably a good thing. I've been looking a little thin lately, don't you think?'

Amber laughed. 'OK, I get the hint. I'll feed you up.'

She was still smiling as he went off in search of his next patient. As she turned to pick up a chart, she saw that Nick had approached the desk. His gaze was on Casey, too.

'You and he seem to be getting on very well,' he said.

'Yes, we are. I like him. He's fun, and he's a good doctor, too.' She was still smiling, but when she looked at Nick, she saw that his expression was brooding.

'Maybe. That's still to be proved.'

She stared at him. Was he still doubtful about the incident with the patient the other day? Did he think Casey had made a mistake?

'I don't see any reason not to take him at face

value,' she murmured. 'He gets on well with everyone here…well, mostly everyone.' Perhaps she couldn't count Nick among those people.

'I think you should be careful around him,' Nick said. 'I heard that he was very taken with a woman and her young son. They aren't with him, by all accounts, but I wouldn't like you to get hurt.'

He walked away from her, and Amber mulled over what he had said. Was it true?

She had thought Casey was footloose and fancy-free, but now she wondered what was going on. It didn't necessarily have to be anything untoward, though, did it?

Anyway, why was Nick concerning himself with her friendships? She didn't query his relationship with Chloe, did she?

CHAPTER FIVE

'YOU should invite that nice doctor to come and have dinner with us,' Amber's mother said. She was applying a coat of polish to Aunt Rose's dining-room table, and now she studiously rubbed it in as though it was the most important thing in the world to get a good shine on the surface. 'He's been so good to you—he rescued you from the fire, and then he went to all that trouble to find a decent builder for you. Not to mention that he fixed your plumbing the other day.'

'You mean, you want me to invite my boss over here?' Amber stared at her mother, open-mouthed. 'I'm not so sure that that would be a good idea.' She put the finishing touches to an arrangement of flowers and moved the crystal vase to a low table.

'Why ever not? Your Aunt Rose doesn't mind. In fact, it was she who thought of it. He sounds like a nice, personable young man and we'd both like to meet him and thank him for helping you out.'

Amber shook her head. 'I'm sure he's much too busy to come and spend time with us.'

'Nonsense. He wasn't too busy to come and look around your cottage with his father, was he? Besides, at the price you've been given for all the work, I wouldn't be surprised if they were doing it at cost. I think he's looking out for your interests. He must have a soft spot for you.'

'So that's it,' Amber said, realisation dawning.

'You two are trying to do a bit of matchmaking, aren't you?' She sent her mother a stern look. 'You can forget all about that. You're on completely the wrong track. And anyway, I'm not interested in getting together with anyone. Besides which, he's already involved with a nurse who works at the hospital. I'm the last person on his mind.'

Her mother looked disappointed, but masked it quickly. 'How can you be so sure of that? You don't get many bosses who will go to so much trouble to help out their colleagues.'

'Well, perhaps this one is different. He's supportive towards everyone—well, mostly everyone, with maybe one or two exceptions.' She remembered what he had said about Casey. She still had no idea whether his doubts had any real foundation.

She gave her mother a thoughtful look. 'I don't know why you bother about trying to fix me up,' she said. 'You haven't had the best of experiences, have you? Kyle's father gave you a lot of heartache, didn't he, and you weren't exactly happy with my father, were you?'

'It doesn't have to mean that all relationships are bad. I knew that your father was a strong-willed man when I married him, but I thought that I could soften him up, given time. It didn't work out that way, unfortunately, but you shouldn't let it colour your judgement. Your father had his faults, it's true, and it was very difficult to live with him, but he simply didn't know how to change.'

'I don't know how you coped for as long as you did. I don't think I would want to live with anyone as authoritarian as he was, but how can you know what you're letting yourself in for until you've fallen into the trap?'

'You can't go on my example. I expect I'm naturally a bit of a pushover. I obviously don't have what it takes to stand up to hard types, but you're different to me. If there's anything you got from your father, it was the ability to fight back.'

Amber winced. 'I hope I'm not like him, in any way. He could only ever see his own point of view, and I hope that I'm more open-minded than that. If there's one thing above all that he taught me, it's that I need to be independent. I don't think I ever want to be subservient to any man.'

She sent her mother a fleeting glance. 'What was Kyle's father like? You hardly ever talk about him, but you must have loved him at one time.'

'He was a strong man, too. I think I must have been drawn to men like that…' Her mother's eyes took on a far-away look. 'But not any more. I've learned my lesson.'

She straightened up from the table and folded the duster. 'He was a soldier. I suppose that's why Kyle went off and joined the army, because he wanted to be like his father, even though he didn't remember him very much. I didn't want him to do it, but I couldn't stand in his way. It wasn't a life that suited me, being a soldier's wife. We moved around a lot, and lived in married quarters, and it was lonely a lot of the time. There was so much worry, too, because the nature of the job meant that he could be hurt at any time.'

'That's what happened, isn't it?'

Her mother nodded. 'He went out on a mission one

day, and he didn't come back. It was the worst day of my life when they came and told me what had happened. No—that's not right. The worst day was when Kyle left and didn't come back. You always feel worse when something happens to your children. They're young and vulnerable and you want the best for them.'

She looked up at Amber and gave a faint smile. 'You mustn't blame me for wanting you to be happy. It's all I've ever wanted.'

Amber went over to her mother and gave her a hug. 'I know. But you mustn't worry about me, and you don't need to try to find ways to fix me up with someone. I'm happy in my work, and now I have the cottage, and I'm going to make something of it. You don't need to watch over me and fret. I'm fine as I am.'

This way, she could guard against ever being hurt the way her mother had been hurt. She needed to keep a protective barrier around herself, a constant reminder that things could go wrong, but only if she let them.

At work, she was plunged straight into action. The paramedics were bringing in people who had been injured in a minor explosion at their workplace, and Amber didn't have time to stop for a moment. As soon as those casualties had been treated, a woman and her baby were brought into A and E.

'They were involved in a car crash,' Chloe said. 'Apparently Mrs Byres was bringing the baby to A and E because she was worried about him, but unfortunately a car hit hers just as she was pulling out onto the main road. She said it was travelling too fast.'

'I'll take a look at her,' Casey said. 'From the sound of it she's suffering from whiplash and bruising. I'll check for internal injuries.'

Amber examined the baby. He was about four weeks old, and she was concerned about his condition. There were no apparent injuries, but he looked dehydrated.

'Did she say what she thought was wrong with the infant? What were his symptoms?'

'Apparently he's dehydrated and he's been vomiting.'

Amber was gently feeling the child's abdomen. 'I think I can feel something, here,' she said. 'Did the mother say whether the vomiting was projectile?'

Chloe checked the notes. 'She doesn't exactly say that, but I think that's what she meant.'

'I'm going to do an ultrasound scan to see what we're dealing with here. In the meantime, he needs fluids to correct the dehydration. I'm going to insert an IV cannula and send blood for urea and electrolytes, glucose and full blood count.' She glanced at Chloe. 'Will you give the paediatrician a call? I think she needs to come and take a look at this baby, and we may need a surgical consult.'

'I'll do that.' Chloe hurried away.

'Are you and Casey managing here?' Amber looked up to find that Nick was looking at the child's chart.

'Yes, I think so. I'm going to examine the child again while he's having a test feed.'

'You're thinking hypertrophic pyloric stenosis?'

Amber nodded. 'If I'm right, he'll need surgery to clear the obstruction of the stomach outlet.'

'It could take several hours before he's ready for that. He needs to be rehydrated first, and you should check for metabolic alkalosis.'

'I will.' She looked at the child. 'Poor little scrap. He's so tiny, isn't he?'

Nick bent over the infant and placed his finger against the child's palm. Instantly the fingers curled and gripped onto him. He smiled. 'Yes, he is, but I don't think you need to worry about him. He should come through this all right, with no complications.'

'I know. It's just that he so tiny, and he looks so vulnerable.'

He turned to Amber. 'You were very gentle with him. I couldn't help noticing that there was a tenderness about you when you looked at him. Have you thought about having a family of your own?'

'Sometimes. I wonder what it would be like to have a child, but I don't know whether it's on the cards for me.'

He sent her a questioning look. 'Why is that? Is there a problem?'

She shook her head. 'It's just something that I feel inside. I haven't seen much happiness from within my own family, and I don't know if things will work out for me. I suppose you could say that I'm ultra-cautious.'

He looked her over, his grey eyes searching her face. 'Things don't always have to be perfect, do they? Chloe hasn't had the best of luck in life, but she has Lucy, and she says that she's the best thing that could have happened to her.'

'Maybe, but Lucy has been ill, hasn't she? I'm not sure whether I could cope with the constant anxiety. Chloe told me this morning that her little girl was frightened and not sleeping well.'

'Lucy's worrying about the robbery. Chloe spoke to the people whose house was ransacked the other day, and they were very upset. The lady of the house lost some jewellery. Some valuable pieces were taken, but there were also some that were very precious to her—a ring that her mother gave her, and a gold locket with pictures of her children inside. The burglars caused a lot of damage, too.'

'It must be very upsetting.' Amber frowned. Nick certainly knew everything that was going on in Chloe's life. It was good that he was there for her, but how deep did his interest go?

She didn't voice her thoughts. Instead she said, 'Why is Lucy worrying about it? Does she think that they'll come to her house?'

'I don't think so. I suppose she's anxious because Chloe has been worried about her ex-husband, and although she's tried to keep it from her daughter, some of her unease must have rubbed off.'

'I hope the police catch whoever is responsible. Perhaps they'll both rest more easily then.'

Casey came over to join them, and Nick turned to face him. 'The mother is more comfortable now,' Casey said, glancing at Amber. 'She's asking about her baby.'

Amber nodded. 'I'll go and have a word with her.'

Chloe came to keep an eye on the infant, and Amber noticed that Nick stood with her for a while, talking to her until the paramedics brought in another patient. Then he went to attend to the emergency.

Amber spoke to the mother who had been injured in the car accident, and gently reassured her. 'We're doing tests to find out exactly what's wrong, but we think that your baby may have an obstruction to the outlet of his stomach, and that's why he's vomiting. If that's the case, we can put that right, but I'll ask the paediatrician to come and have a word with you, and explain things more fully. You did the right thing, bringing your baby here.'

'I knew that he was ill, that something was wrong.' The young woman was pale, and her bruises were obviously making her uncomfortable, but she appeared relieved now that something was being done to help her child. 'He couldn't keep any of his feeds down, and he wasn't thriving. I knew he couldn't go on like that.'

As soon as she had made sure that the infant was in a stable condition, Amber went outside to take a break. There was a small paved area at the back of the A and E unit, and she went there now and sat on the wooden bench where she could take a breath of air. It was late springtime, almost summer, and the sky was a pale blue, and it was pleasant to sit here for a while and look at the distant trees whose branches were weighted down with blossom.

After a few minutes, Casey came and joined her there. 'I wonder why we do this job sometimes,' he said. 'You can have mornings where you scarcely get a minute to breathe, and you feel as though your body's screaming for a rest.'

She gave him an oblique glance. 'You were on call

last night, weren't you? Lack of sleep tends to make you feel like that. Did you get any sleep at all?'

'A couple of hours, I think.' He grimaced. 'I suppose I shouldn't complain. Chloe reckons she gets a few nights like that when Lucy is troubled.'

'It can't be easy for her, can it? Being a single mother means you have to take on the whole burden of keeping a home together and caring for your offspring.'

'I expect that's why she's turned to Nick for help. I hope she doesn't come to rely on him too much.'

Amber frowned. 'What do you mean? Surely it's a good thing that she has someone to support her?'

'It can be. But I've been there myself. I know that those kinds of situations can be fraught with problems.'

'You mean that you've been a single parent, or that you've been married and it didn't work out?'

He shook his head. 'Neither of those. I was very friendly with a girl who had a small child. She gave me a place to stay for a while, and I think she began to see me as a father for the boy. I knew then that I had to move out. I wasn't sure that I was right for her, that things would work out between us, and I didn't want the boy to come to rely on me. I thought it would be too painful for him if I stayed on and then later changed my mind and decided to leave.'

'I'm sorry. Was it bad when you left?'

He grimaced. 'I tried to make it as easy as I could. I told them that I was leaving, and then I popped back to see them every so often, so that it wasn't such a wrench for the child. I think he was all right about it, but Sarah was upset.'

'Do you still go back and see them?'

'No. I've made a clean break now.'

Amber didn't say anything, but in her mind she was troubled. Casey must have noticed because he said, 'What's wrong? You seem upset. Is it something that I've said?'

'No, it isn't that. I was just thinking that a clean break could be very painful for those left behind. You hear about missing people who never go back home because they are afraid of what waits for them, of what reaction they'll get. And all the time their families are praying for them to come back.'

'You make it sound as though you've experienced something like that. Has it happened to you?'

She nodded. 'My brother left home a long time ago. I keep wishing that I could find him and talk to him and ask him to come back.'

'I suppose it depends if the reasons for his leaving have changed at all. A lot of young people leave home because they can't get on with their parents, because they are arguing all the time. If there's a lot of bad feeling, the thought of actually going back can be insurmountable.'

She gave him a sideways look. 'Now you sound as if you know all about that, as though you've been through it.'

'I've worked with youngsters who left home for one reason or another. Going back isn't always the answer. Sometimes they have to move on and make a new life for themselves.'

'It sounds as though you've had quite a lot of different experiences before you became a doctor.'

He made a wry smile. 'I was a late developer. It

took me a while to make up my mind what I wanted to do.'

'And now everything is working out for you, is it?'

'Mostly.'

'But…this girl and her child, you don't know how things are working out for them? You're definitely not going back to them?'

His mouth made a straight line. 'No. I still think it's better this way, even though Sarah has taken it badly. I think she was hoping that we had a future together. People round about were beginning to think that we were a couple.'

'Ah…I see.' Amber recalled what Nick had said. 'That would explain it.'

He sent puzzled look. 'Explain what?'

'The rumour mill has been working overtime. People have the idea that you were deeply involved.'

'Not any more. I think I'm a little afraid of the responsibility.'

Nick's deep voice came to them from the entrance to the A and E unit. 'We've a couple of accident victims coming in. I need you two back in here.'

'We're on our way.' Amber stood up and headed back to work. Casey followed.

It was clear from the start that they were fighting a losing battle, but even so Amber did what she could to save her patient, a young man who had been thrown off his motorbike. He was unconscious and bleeding heavily, and his injuries were so severe that she couldn't keep up with the blood loss. She called for help and Nick came to work alongside her.

He stemmed the flow where he could and Amber was amazed at his skill. She didn't think she would have been able to do what he did with such efficiency or such sureness of touch. They pumped blood into their patient but, no matter how hard they worked, the flow was unremitting.

Finally, just as Amber thought they might be winning, the young man went into cardiac arrest.

They worked as a team to bring him back. Nick said, 'I'm going to defibrillate. Charging, stand back.'

He tried several times, but in the end it was to no avail. Amber could see the wretchedness in his expression. He said, 'I think we've done all that we can for him. We've been working on him for more than an hour. He's gone. Does everyone agree?'

Amber felt numb inside. They had all done what they could, but it had been no use. His was such a young life, and it was such a waste to see him die in hospital. She nodded along with everyone else, and then she stood back and wondered what they were going to say to his parents.

Nick took care of it. After he had changed out of his scrubs and cleaned himself up, she saw him go in search of them. He took them to one side and spoke quietly with them, and then they disappeared into the relatives' room.

Casey said, 'We managed to save the passenger on the bike. His injuries were bad, but he'll pull through.'

'You did well,' she muttered. She had changed out of her own scrubs and was walking back to the reception desk. 'I wish we could have done more for his companion.'

She turned away and saw that a couple of police

officers had appeared in the doorway. 'Can I help you?' Chloe was saying to them.

'We wanted to interview those two young men who were brought in,' one of the officers said. 'They stole a motorbike and we had to give chase.'

Amber said stiffly, 'I doubt that they'll be stealing any more motorbikes.' The officer looked at her blankly, and she walked away from him and let Chloe answer his questions.

Nick was coming out of the relatives' room as she picked up a chart. He signalled to Mandy to go and sit with the people who were in there, and then he caught up with Amber. She was simply staring into space, and he removed the chart from her hand, took hold of her arm and led her away towards the doctors' lounge.

'There are more patients coming in,' she said. 'I should go and get ready for them.'

'No, you won't. You'll stay here and take a few minutes. I know that you're upset, but you did everything that you could back there—we all did. We had no chance from the outset, but we did what we had to do.'

'It wasn't enough.' Tears welled up in her eyes and she tried to blink them away.

His arms came around her and he turned her to face him. 'It happens,' he said. 'None of us wants things to turn out this way, but it happens sometimes.'

He drew her to him and wrapped her in his embrace. She rested her cheek against the lapel of his jacket, and he stood with her and soothed her until she quieted.

'They were so young,' she said unevenly. 'They

were just starting out on life, and now one of them is dead and the other will carry the scars for the rest of his life.'

'Think about all those lives that you've saved over the years,' he said. 'They all have a chance because of you, because you were there when they needed your help. You have to try to put this behind you. If you don't, you won't be able to carry on. The sadness will overwhelm you.'

'Is that how you get through it?' she asked, looking up at him. 'You think of the ones you've saved?'

'I try to. It's always worse when the patient is young. It hits us all, but you have to remember that if you weren't here and able to do your job, the toll would be worse. You can make a difference, but you have to move on.'

'I'll be all right now,' she said huskily. 'Thank you for listening to me.'

'I need you,' he said softly. 'I need you working alongside me and on my team. I can't have you falling by the wayside.'

His fingers traced the outline of her face, and then he cupped his hand beneath her chin and tilted her jaw slightly so that her mouth was just a fraction away from his. He bent his head to her and kissed her, a feather-light kiss that brushed her lips and lit a fire within her.

Her senses erupted in confusion. The warmth of his body caressed her and comforted her, and his grey eyes meshed with hers as though he would see right into her soul.

She didn't know how to respond. Her lips ached for him. She wanted him to kiss her again, and she longed to lean on him to have him shelter her from the brittle touch of life, but she was afraid. She was unsure of what to do, and she gazed at him with troubled eyes.

He must have sensed her uncertainty because he kissed her again, more firmly this time, and she closed her eyes and absorbed the sweet, inviting query in that kiss.

It was only when she heard the sound of trolleys clattering in the distance that she came back to the full realisation of where she was and what she was doing.

She pulled away from him, and he let her go, looking at her with a kind of bemusement, as though he too had been caught up in something surreal.

'I wasn't thinking straight,' she mumbled. 'I think everything has got a little bit out of hand.'

'You're right, of course,' he said. His voice had a roughened edge, and she wasn't sure what to make of his expression. 'I shouldn't have done that. My only excuse is that the events of the day affect us all, and maybe our emotions tend to run out of control. Perhaps we all sometimes act in ways that are too primitive to countenance. I'm sorry.'

Reluctantly, he let her go, and she wondered if that was the truth of it, that he too had been affected by the tragedy in such a way that their kiss had been one of mutual comfort.

'We'll just forget it, shall we?' Her gaze was questioning.

'I think that would be for the best. We'll agree that it never happened.'

CHAPTER SIX

'I'M JUST about ready to put the worktop in place,' Casey said, 'and then it'll really look as though you have a proper kitchen.' He looked around the room with satisfaction. 'It's coming on, don't you think?'

'It looks much better than I ever imagined,' Amber agreed. She handed him a mug of coffee, then stood beside him and looked at the neat units that made up her kitchen. 'I'm really grateful to you for all that you've done. You've worked so hard these last few days and it can't have been easy for you. After all, you put in a full day in A and E before you come here, and this must be the fourth day in a row. I don't know how you have the stamina to keep it up.'

'The same goes for you.' He took a sip of the hot liquid. 'You haven't been sitting around with your feet up, have you? While I've been working, you've been fixing tiles in the bathroom and painting the woodwork throughout the house. You've made a really good job of it.'

'Thanks. Actually, the tiling wasn't my handiwork. It's not something I've done before, fixing tiles, and I was nervous that I wouldn't get it right. I made a start just after the new bathroom had been fitted, but Nick happened to come along that day, and he took over from me. To be honest, I don't think he thought much of my efforts, and he decided it needed to be done properly.'

Casey laughed. 'You're telling me that our boss actually came here and fitted your tiles?'

She nodded. 'I told him that I would be able to manage, but he took no notice, and I was worried about him getting his clothes messed up. He was wearing really good trousers and a jacket, but he just took the jacket off and rolled up his shirtsleeves and got on with it.'

'I'm amazed. He's done a really good job.'

'Yes. I'm more than pleased with the finish. He said that he used to go around with his father, overseeing the properties that he had bought, and his father would always take an active part in the renovations. To be honest, I think it was more of a hobby with Nick. He said that it takes his mind off the everyday trauma that we see at the hospital.'

'Why did he come along here in the first place? Do you and he have something going?'

'Good heavens, no.' Amber couldn't help the quick flush of heat that ran along her cheekbones. 'He just came to make sure that everything was moving along all right. He wanted to check that everything is going to plan.'

In truth, she had been startled to see Nick arrive on her doorstep, but he had been perfectly relaxed and there had been no hint that anything had gone on between them. He had said that he had told his father he would keep an eye on things, and that was how it seemed. He was simply there to see that the builders were keeping to schedule.

'Is there much more to be done before you have everything as you want it in the cottage?'

'The builders are working on the living room, at

the moment, and then there's the fireplace to be fitted.
I'm amazed at how quickly they've got on with everything.'

'Are the costs working out all right for you?' He
suddenly stopped. 'Sorry, that's really none of my
business.'

'I don't mind.' Somehow, it was easy to talk to
Casey. There was none of the inner tension that she
felt whenever she was near Nick. With Casey, she
was completely casual and laid-back. 'I've taken out
an extra mortgage to cover the building work, and
I'm using my savings for the kitchen units and the
bathroom. So far, I'm just about managing to keep
my head above water.'

'That's good.' He put down his empty coffee-mug,
and said, 'I'll get back to work. It shouldn't take long
now.'

'I'll give you a hand.'

Together, they manoeuvred the worktop into place.
It was a pleasing finish, a pale golden oak wood block
surface that accentuated the perfect lines of the
kitchen.

Casey was checking things over when the front
doorbell rang. Amber frowned, and glanced at her
watch. 'I wonder who that can be?'

'You're not expecting anyone?'

Amber shook her head and went to open the door.
Nick was there, and she drew back in surprise, saying,
'Nick...I didn't think I would see you until tomorrow,
at work.'

'I just came to drop off the key to your shed. Tony
put some equipment away this afternoon and walked
away with key by mistake. He thought you might

need it because you keep your paint pots in there, and he knows you've been busy working on the woodwork. He was going to make a special journey and bring it himself, but I said I was going to be passing by this way.'

'I wondered what had happened. I wasn't doing any painting tonight, but thanks all the same.' She pulled the door open and invited him in. 'Do you have time to come in for a coffee?'

'Thanks, I'd like that. I'm supposed to be having supper with my parents, but they're not expecting me for half an hour or so.'

She showed him into the kitchen, and he and Casey stared at each other for a moment. She said, 'Casey's been fixing my kitchen cupboards for me. He's made a wonderful job of them, hasn't he?'

Nick glanced around. 'It's very impressive. I like the cream colour and the contrast of the worktops. The floor looks good, too. The wood finish complements everything.'

He looked at Casey. 'Have you done this sort of thing before?'

'A couple of times. I bought an old terraced house a few years back and tried to make something of it, and then I put in a kitchen for my ex-girlfriend.' He gave Nick direct look. 'Amber tells me that your father does quite a lot of work on his properties.'

'That's true. He does, initially. I've learned a lot from going with him to view the properties. There's always something that needs to be done to make them fit in with his ideas of what makes them habitable. He keeps the tenants in mind, and tries to make sure that there is a good finish, but at the same time there should be nothing that's too expensive to replace if it should be damaged.'

The two men were making polite conversation, but Amber could feel the tension in the atmosphere. She busied herself pouring coffee, and then tried to smooth things over. She had no idea why they should be sparring with each other, but there was a definite antagonism between them.

She said, 'I feel that I've been really lucky to have so much help with this house. When I started out, I thought I had a marathon task ahead of me, but with all the help that you've both given me it's been so much easier. I'm really grateful to both of you.'

'You're welcome.' Casey smiled at her and put an arm around her shoulders. 'I've been glad to help out. Considering what this place was like when you first moved in, it's turned into a minor miracle.'

'That's true. It looks very different now.'

Casey said, 'Nick was talking about his father and what he does. What about your father? You hardly ever mention him, but I should imagine he must be proud of what you've achieved here. Does he come and help out sometimes?'

Amber shook her head. 'I don't really have anything to do with my father these days. As to him ever coming here…I shudder at the thought. He'd be telling me that I'd done everything wrong, and I can imagine him ordering me to rip everything out and do it his way, the proper way. He always has to put his stamp on things. He was never satisfied with anything that I did. He wasn't an easy man to live with.'

Casey frowned. 'That must be very hard for you.

You're older now, though, and surely he can't tell you what to do?'

'I wouldn't put it past him to try…not that I would give him the chance nowadays.'

'It sounds as though at least you have managed to escape. I suppose getting a place of your own was a good move. What about your mother? How does she cope?'

'She doesn't have to these days. She divorced my father some years ago. To be honest, she told me that she only stayed with him until she felt that I was old enough to accept the rift.'

'I'm sorry.' Casey frowned. 'I didn't mean to revive any bad memories. I can see that it still bothers you.'

Nick glanced her way. 'Does it still bother you?'

Amber gave a negligent shrug. 'For the most part, I try not to think about my parents' marriage. I would have been happier if my mother had divorced him long before she did.'

Casey said, 'I hadn't realised that your parents had split up. No matter what the reasons, it must be hard for everyone concerned.' He looked around, uncertainly, as though he still felt uncomfortable that he had been the one to stir up the past. 'I really should be getting off home now. If you need me to come and help with anything else, though, you only have to say.'

He moved away from her, and went to collect his jacket from the back of a chair. 'Thanks for the meal, Amber. It was delicious. I'll see you at work tomorrow.' He nodded to Nick.

Amber saw him out, and then went back to the

kitchen. Nick was looking around at the bare walls, his glance gliding over the neat wall units and the newly fitted breakfast bar. He turned as she came into the room.

'You get on very well with him, don't you?' he murmured.

She nodded. 'He's been a great friend to me. I'd still be struggling with all this if it hadn't been for you and him.'

'Maybe. It seems to me that you're more resilient than you give yourself credit for. From what I've seen, you've painted and decorated, you've made curtains and soft furnishings, and generally added your own special touch to the place.'

She frowned. 'How did you know that I'd made the curtains and soft furnishings? Do they look home-made?'

His mouth made a wry smile. 'No, they don't. I saw the material next to your sewing machine the other day. I think you've made a very professional job of everything.'

'Thank you.'

He looked around once more and frowned. 'Are you planning on tiling in here?' he asked. 'Or are you going to leave it with a paint finish?'

'I've already bought the tiles,' she said. 'I'll have a go at putting them up next week.'

'Judging by your efforts in the bathroom,' he murmured, 'that's one thing that you're not particularly good at. I think you had better leave that to me. I'll come and fix them for you.'

'I don't want to impose on you,' she objected. 'I know you're a busy man.' She hesitated. 'Besides, I wouldn't like you to get the wrong impression of me. I know when we first met I may have seemed as though I'm not always at my best, but I do have some skills, and I do manage to learn as I go on.'

He made a crooked smile. 'I know that. I know that you always aim to do the very best you can, but perhaps you should accept that some things are just not your forte.'

She said cautiously, 'I think that time is the worst enemy. There is always so much that needs to be done.'

He swallowed his coffee and said, 'I know things haven't been easy for you lately, with your mother being ill and all this work going on at the cottage. Then you have to put in a full day's work at the hospital, and that in itself can take its toll.' His glance searched her face. 'Is your mother feeling any better? I know you said that she was going to have her blood pressure monitored.'

'Her appointment hasn't come through yet. I've tried to get them to hurry it up, but the waiting lists are quite long. I'm worried about her headaches and the symptoms that go along with them. I just feel that she needs to receive treatment before things get out of hand.'

'I'll have a word with the specialist, if you like. There might be a slot in his list if someone rings to say they're not able to make their appointment.'

'That would certainly be an answer.' She made a face. 'I'm not sure quite why I'm so anxious—perhaps it's just instinct, but I have a nagging feeling that something is badly wrong. I won't feel happy until I know that she's had a thorough check-up.'

'It could just be that she's under stress, I suppose. You said that she was worrying about your brother. I know it's a problem that has gone on for a long while, but perhaps she's reached that time of life when things are weighing her down more.'

'You could be right. I wish that there was something more I could do to find him. The advertisement in the paper didn't lead to anything, and I've tried the Salvation Army and all the other usual routes.'

'What about the army itself? You said he joined up, so they must have some record of his whereabouts.'

She shook her head. 'Apparently not. They said he was with them for a number of years, and they had a record of his postings abroad, but then there was a foul-up at the records office—a problem with the computers and the paperwork—and the trail just seems to have ended.'

'I'm sorry. That was bad luck.' He moved towards her and put his arm around her. 'You could maybe try the electoral registers in all the local towns hereabouts. It might take quite a while, but it's a start.'

Her face lit up. 'That's a really good idea. I'm not sure how much of that sort of tracing has already been done, but I can find out, and work on the rest.' She gazed into his eyes, and for a moment, for a short breath of time, there was an answering warmth in his glance. She almost reached up to him, her mouth softening, ready for his kiss.

Just in time, though, she collected herself and moved back from him. Lowering her head, she said, 'I'll go and organise that tomorrow.'

He straightened and put his cup down on the new

worktop. 'I should go,' he said. 'I'll see you in the morning.'

She saw him to the door, and watched as he climbed into his sleek car. He drove away without a backward glance, and she went back into the house and felt the emptiness surround her. It was lonely without him here.

Next morning, she found that they were busier than usual in the department. She was rushed off her feet for the first few hours, and she found herself longing for a break.

'Chloe, would you come and help me with this patient, please?' Amber called when she saw the nurse heading towards the supplies room. 'I need you to dress a wound for me.'

'I'll be just a moment,' the nurse answered. 'I have to look for some more syringes, and I don't have the right size tubing.'

'As soon as you can,' Amber agreed.

Chloe looked distracted this morning, and Amber wondered whether there had been any more untoward events close to home. On her way to find her next patient, she hurried along the corridor and almost stumbled over little Lucy, who was coming out of the doctors' lounge.

'Lucy,' Amber said. 'Are you feeling poorly again? Do you have to go and see the doctor today?'

Lucy shook her head, and her curls danced, shining in the light from the overhead lamp. 'I was at nursery school, but I wanted to come and see Mummy. She said that she'd take me to get a burger, but she's not ready yet.'

'A burger? That sounds yummy. Is that your favourite food?'

'No, but you get a toy if you have a burger and fries. I just like puddings, but Mummy says I can't have puddings all the time.'

Amber smiled. 'Your mummy's probably right about that, but I know what you mean. I like puddings as well. I like apple pie and ice cream.'

'My favourite,' said a deep masculine voice from behind her, 'is cherry pie with lashings of custard.'

Amber turned around and saw that Nick had appeared in the corridor. He hunkered down beside the child and said, 'I think we'd better take you where someone can look after you. Your mummy's busy just now, and I think she might be a little worried if she realises that you're wandering about. Let's see if we can find our desk clerk. Tim might be able to watch over you for a little while. I think he keeps some soft toys under the desk. If you're really good, he might let you play with them.'

He straightened up and took the little girl by the hand, nodding to Amber as if to say that he would look out for her. Amber watched the pair of them go off together to find the desk clerk.

Seeing Nick at her house last night had brought all Amber's warring emotions to the surface once more. These last few days he had worked alongside her and made no mention of what had happened between them that day when he had kissed her. She was glad of that, because she was totally out of her depth where he was concerned.

On the one hand, she was energised to have him close by, and she was constantly aware of him. It made the blood sizzle in her veins, knowing that there might be some spark between them, but it would never do to physically acknowledge that, would it? He was her boss, he was in charge of this whole department, and it would have been more than awkward if there had been any suggestion of something going on.

People seemed to accept that he was supportive to Chloe and that there might even be something more between them, but it wouldn't do for Amber to intrude on that relationship.

'Amber, will you come in here?' Casey's tone sounded urgent, and Amber swivelled around and hurried over to him. He was working in the treatment room just off the corridor, and he must have seen her walk by.

'What's the problem?' she asked. Going into the room, she saw that he was treating a man of around fifty years old. The man was receiving oxygen, and Casey had established intravenous access. The patient's relatives stood to one side, looking anxious.

'He was brought in suffering from atrial fibrillation,' Casey said. He lowered his voice and added, 'I've followed all the protocols, but his condition is deteriorating. He's showing signs of agitation and visual disturbances, and he's been vomiting. I'm concerned about his cardiac rhythm.'

'Are you treating him with digoxin?'

'Yes, by infusion, but things are not happening as I expected. I'm afraid that something's gone wrong.'

'Could it be the dosage?'

'I don't see how. Mandy checked it with me.'

Mandy, who was assisting, nodded agreement.

JOANNA NEIL 113

'Casey did everything that he should. I just don't understand what's causing the patient's response.'

'I think we need to get some blood levels anyway, and we should let Nick know what's happening.'

'Did I hear my name mentioned?' Nick appeared in the doorway. He glanced at the patient, and at the monitors, and Casey briefed him on what was going on.

'It sounds like a digoxin overload. Stop the infusion right now, and give him intravenous potassium and dextrose. Continue with the ECG monitoring. We need to get him back to sinus rhythm. You should try magnesium as well. Keep him on this therapy for at least an hour.'

Casey went over to the infusion pump. He stared at it, and Amber said, 'What is it?'

'It looks as though he's received the whole of the infusion in a matter of minutes,' he muttered. 'That shouldn't have happened.'

Nick glanced their way. 'Remove the pump and get another one.'

The man's wife stepped forward. 'What's happening? What's wrong?'

Nick took her to one side and spoke to her quietly. Amber heard him explain that her husband was suffering from an abnormal cardiac rhythm and that they were doing everything they could to restore his heart to a normal rhythm. The woman looked agitated. She turned to the man who had accompanied her, and they spoke together in an undertone. Amber guessed that the man was the patient's brother.

Casey, meanwhile, did as Nick had suggested and removed the infusion pump. Nick took charge of it.

He turned to Mandy and said, 'I think it would be better if Mrs Ramsay and her brother were to go and wait in the relatives' room. They might appreciate a cup of tea.'

Mandy led the couple away, and Nick left the treatment room with the pump. He came back in a matter of minutes and said, 'How's it going?'

'We're still having problems.' Amber stared at the monitors anxiously.

'We need to give him digoxin antibodies as soon as possible,' Nick said. 'It should rapidly correct the arrhythmia and the hyperkalaemia.'

'Do we have any?' Amber said in a low voice. 'I thought hospitals rarely stocked it? It's supposed to be expensive, isn't it?'

'That's true, but I've sent for emergency supplies. It should be here within the next half-hour. In the meantime, we'll try to control the metabolic acidosis with sodium bicarbonate.'

Amber hoped that their patient could hold on for that length of time. Acute digoxin poisoning could be fatal. Somehow, though, with Nick working alongside them, she felt that the man had the best chance of survival. Nick would make sure that everything possible was done to keep him alive.

'Should we try cardiac pacing?' Casey asked.

Nick shook his head. 'We'll leave that as a last resort. It may not be effective, and it could be dangerous at this stage. Keep monitoring him and be prepared to use atropine.'

They were still working with their patient when the digoxin antibodies arrived. 'I've worked out the dose required according to the patient's body weight and plasma digoxin concentration,' Nick said. 'Let's see if we can get him back on track.'

It was another hour before they were satisfied that their patient was going to pull through. Amber breathed a quiet sigh of relief. It had been touch and go, but Nick had taken the lead the whole time, and he had worked with supreme efficiency and skill. She couldn't help but respect him as a doctor.

Even so, she worried about the aftermath of this event. She was sure that there would be an inquisition about what had gone wrong, and she couldn't help worrying for Casey.

'Let's get back to work,' Nick said. 'There are other patients to be seen.'

Amber moved reluctantly towards the desk. She busied herself writing up her notes before she picked up her next chart. It was a worrying situation. She doubted that Nick would leave things as they were, but she had no idea what he was going to do. He spoke to Casey as they left the treatment room, and after a few minutes Casey came to join her by the desk.

'What did he say?' she asked. 'Has he accepted your version of what happened?'

'I think so. I don't really know, to be honest. He said that he would go and talk to the relatives, and he wants to talk to me later, at the end of the shift.'

'I don't understand how we can have two infusion pumps that aren't working properly,' Amber said. 'To have one go wrong could be a fluke, but to find that two of them aren't working properly is unheard-of.'

'I think that's the whole point, though. I've just been along to the office where Nick put the infusion pump and I checked the number on it. It's the same one that should have been sent to Biomedical Engineering. It obviously didn't get taken out of action in the first place.' He shook his head in bewilderment. 'I don't know how that can have happened, because I put it to one side, and I stuck a label on it ready for the porter to come and collect it.'

'Didn't you ask Chloe to deal with it at the time?'

'Yes, I did. I asked her to make sure that it went down to the bio-med department. I've no idea what went wrong. I know that we were both busy then. Either of us could easily have been distracted, but I do remember putting it to one side.'

'Perhaps you should talk to her and find out.'

'I will.'

Amber went in search of her next patient, and she didn't see much more of Nick through the afternoon. He was busy dealing with other emergencies, and she was on edge the whole time, worrying about what was going to happen to Casey.

'Amber,' Nick said towards the end of the afternoon, 'can I have a word with you for a moment?' He was coming out of one of the treatment rooms just as she was getting ready to look in on a patient.

She stopped. 'Of course. Is it about what happened earlier?'

He looked at her quizzically. 'You mean with the patient who had the digoxin overdose? Are you concerned about that? Is there something you wanted to tell me about the incident?'

She sent him a troubled look. 'Only that I'm sure Casey did nothing wrong. He checked the dosage of the medication and he followed all the correct procedures. Mandy will confirm that. I think it was an accident, something that couldn't have been prevented.'

He made a wry smile. 'You're very loyal to him. I know he's a friend, as well as a colleague, and it's good for him that you're willing to stand by him. It says a lot about your friendship.'

'I think it's important to support colleagues. I'm sure that you would do the same, wouldn't you?'

'The thing is,' he said cautiously, 'I have to oversee everything that happens here. Ultimately I'm responsible for the way the department operates. I can't afford to go on sentiment alone.'

Her expression faltered. 'Does that mean he's in trouble?'

'It means that I have to talk to everyone concerned before I make any decisions about what's to happen.' He paused. 'Actually, that wasn't what I wanted to speak to you about. It was about your mother and her appointment with the specialist.'

'Oh, I see. I didn't think you would have done anything about that yet.' She looked at him questioningly.

'I had a word with the appointments clerk at lunchtime. She said that someone cancelled for this afternoon, and they can see your mother today if she can get along to the clinic. It's only to fit her with the monitor, but once they have an idea of what's happening with her blood pressure over a twenty-four-hour period, the specialist can decide what needs to be done. If they find that there is any urgency in her situation, the consultant will see her within a very short time.'

'Thank you for that. I'm so relieved. I'll give her a ring and let her know. It's been nagging away at the back of my mind all the time, and it takes a load off me to know that she's going to be seen very soon.' She smiled at him, and his mouth relaxed, his eyes growing warm as he ran his gaze over her.

'I'm glad to be of help.'

He turned away as Mandy caught his attention, asking for him to come and look at someone who was convulsing, and Amber went to make her phone call and then went back to the treatment room to monitor her own patient.

At the end of the day, when it was time for her to go home, she waited around in the doctors' lounge, wondering anxiously how Casey was getting on. He had been in Nick's office for at least fifteen minutes, and she was desperate to know whether the situation had been resolved.

'How did it go?' She glanced at Casey as he came into the room.

He shook his head. 'There's going to be an inquiry,' he said. His face was pale, and she could tell that he was devastated by the news. 'It will be a day or so before I know the worst, but Nick says he has to look into the mix-up over the infusion pump. If it had gone to the engineering department after the fault was first discovered, there would have been no problem, but because it was brought back into service, because it had never been taken out of service, there's a question of negligence. I'm under a cloud until it's all sorted out.'

She went over to him and touched his arm. 'Casey,

I'm so sorry. I'm sure that you did nothing wrong. If there's anything I can do, anything at all…'

'Thanks,' he said. 'It's good to know that you have faith in me, at least.'

'Do you want to stay and talk? Perhaps we can work something out between us?'

He reached for his jacket. 'No, you get off home. I think I just need to be alone for a while to think things through. I'll see you here tomorrow.' He gave a faint smile that had no humour in it. 'At least I haven't been suspended yet.'

He went out, and Amber pulled on her own jacket and followed him. By the time she had reached the corridor, he had already gone out through the double doors. Nick came out of his office, and she turned hesitantly towards him.

She said, 'I've just spoken to Casey. He told me that there is to be an inquiry.' She stared at him, her eyes troubled. 'Couldn't you have dealt with it on your own, in an informal way? Why does it have to be brought out into the open?'

'I had no choice,' he said. 'The relatives have made a complaint. They went straight to management and said that they believe there had been malpractice of some sort. If they hadn't done that, perhaps I could have sorted it out here in the unit, but now I'm afraid it has to be official.'

Her gaze never left his face. Her eyes were troubled, her expression filled with dismay.

'I'm sorry,' he said. 'I didn't want things to turn out this way.'

He closed his office door, and began to move purposefully along the corridor. Perhaps he expected her to walk with him, but she stared after him, her heart full of conflicting emotions.

He was such a strong, unbending man. As a doctor, he was among the best, and she respected him for the way he treated his patients with compassion and expertise. As a man he was without equal in her eyes, and she had found herself being drawn to him more and more as the weeks had gone by.

Now everything was going wrong and it troubled her that she felt this way. How could she have feelings for a man who could hurt the people she cared about?

CHAPTER SEVEN

'TRY to keep the oxygen mask in place, Mrs Benson. You need it there so that your chest will start to feel better.' Amber adjusted the mask and then said, 'Now, I just need you to lean forward a little while I listen to your chest.' Amber signalled to Chloe to come and help support the woman while she passed the stethoscope over her patient's back. 'Just breathe in as deeply you can.'

Amber listened carefully and heard a patch of inspiratory crackles. 'All right,' she murmured. 'You can lie back and rest now.' She folded away her stethoscope.

To Chloe, she said, 'Perhaps one or two more pillows will help make her feel more comfortable.'

Chloe nodded, and when the nurse had finished attending to Mrs Benson, Amber added, 'We'll get a chest X-ray, and I want to check blood gases and peak flow. We'll monitor her respiratory rate, pulse and blood pressure.'

Turning back to her patient, Amber said, 'I know that it hurts you to breathe, so I'm going to prescribe something for the pain. We'll give you antibiotics as well, and I'm going to add some nebulised salbutamol to your oxygen. That should help you to start feeling much better very soon.'

'What's wrong with me?' Mrs Benson managed to ask.

'I believe that you're suffering from pneumonia,' Amber said. 'You're very unwell, so it's best if we admit you to hospital for a few days, or at least until we have the infection under control. I hope you will be feeling more comfortable before too long.'

She spoke to the patient for a moment or two longer, answering her questions and reassuring her, and then she moved away from the bedside and went to write up her forms. Chloe followed shortly afterwards.

'I'll go and get things set up for the salbutamol,' she said.

'Thanks.' Amber glanced at her. 'Are you all right? You've been very quiet this morning.'

'I'm a little worried about Lucy,' she said. 'She isn't in school today, and I have a friend looking after her. I'm afraid that she has another chest infection.'

'Have you seen your family doctor?'

'She's going to call in some time today. I called the locum last night, and he prescribed antibiotics. I'll feel happier when my GP has been to see her.'

'I'm sure you will. I'm sorry Lucy is poorly again. She's not having a very easy time of it just lately, is she?'

'No. I'm hoping that I'll be able to get off work early today. It's worrying, being at work, knowing that she is unwell.'

'I'm surprised that you're here at all,' Amber said with a frown. 'I'm sure Nick would let you take time off to be with her. Have you asked him?'

'Not yet. I was worried about this inquiry over the infusion pump. I know there's going to be a management meeting some time this morning, and I'm a little bit anxious about the outcome. I don't know whether I'll be called to make a statement.'

'I'm sure Nick would have phoned you at home to let you know.'

'Maybe. I just need to know what's happening.'

Amber could understand why Chloe was feeling anxious. She remembered seeing Casey talk to her about the infusion pump the first time it had gone wrong, and Amber was fairly sure that he had asked Chloe to see that it was removed and sent to Biomedical Engineering.

Amber was concerned to know the outcome, too. It didn't seem fair that Casey should be taking the blame for something that was possibly a joint responsibility.

Later, when she was writing up forms for lab tests, she caught sight of Nick returning from the meeting. She saw that he stopped to talk to Casey, drawing him away from the patient he was attending. They spoke quietly for a few minutes, and Amber wished that she knew what was going on.

When Nick moved on, though, she saw that Casey was simply standing there, by the treatment room, looking stunned.

Nick came over to the desk and she said, 'Is there any news about the inquiry? What's going to happen about the incident with the patient yesterday?'

He nodded. 'The inquiry is going to go ahead within the next few days. At least it should be dealt with fairly swiftly.'

'That's probably for the best. As it is, Casey looks terrible. Whatever it was that you said to him must have been upsetting. Does it look bad for him? Could you not put in a good word for him and smooth his way?'

'It isn't quite as simple as that. As to the rest, you'll have to ask him what happened. It's not for me to say.' His glance trailed over her. 'I did what I could, Amber, but in the end the decision was made by the management chiefs. They have to protect themselves and the hospital from lawsuits.'

Amber frowned. 'What about Chloe? Are you going to talk to her as well? I know that she's worrying about it.'

'I don't think she has any particular cause to worry. Someone will speak to her in due course, I expect, but it probably won't be me. I won't be the one conducting the investigation, although I could be called to give evidence.'

Amber stared at him. 'I don't understand. Why isn't Chloe under the same threat as Casey? They were both involved, weren't they? I don't believe either of them did anything wrong, but why should Casey be the only one to be in trouble? Are you protecting Chloe at Casey's expense?'

Nick's eyes narrowed on her. 'I think you know better than to be asking me that. It isn't a question of taking sides. I know that you're very fond of Casey, but you have to understand that I have to be seen to be totally impartial. Even so, no matter what you think, I've done my best to protect Casey. In the end, though, he's the one who carries the ultimate responsibility for the mistake, not Chloe.'

'But you know that he's not the only one involved. Why should he have to take it all on his back? He's new here, and it's going to look as if he was untried and untested, and that's not going to look good for him, is it? You can't just let him take the blame. You need to support him.'

'Amber, I'll do whatever I can to help him. I know that you're worried, but you have to trust that everything will be done properly. If I can absolve him from all responsibility, I will, but I can't make any promises at this stage. You have to try to have faith in me.'

He walked away, heading towards one of the treatment rooms, and Amber stared after him. That was what it came down to, wasn't it? Did she trust him? She wanted to, but at the back of her mind she wasn't sure whether he would try to protect Chloe at all costs.

She looked down at the blood-test forms she was holding. Everything had gone out of her mind in the last few minutes, but now she pulled herself together and went to put them in the tray from where they would be collected and sent to the laboratory. Then she went in search of Casey.

He was in the doctors' lounge, staring out of the window that looked out over the hospital grounds. She said, 'What happened? I saw Nick talking to you.'

He turned to face her. 'It's what I expected. I'm going to be suspended until the inquiry is over. I have to clear out my locker.'

'Oh, no… I'm so sorry.' She touched his arm in a gesture of sympathy. 'They'll come to realise that you did nothing wrong. You told me that you put a label on the pump, saying that it might be faulty, and you put it to one side to be collected, didn't you, and you asked Chloe to follow it up? Something went wrong, but it wasn't your fault, I'm sure of it.'

His expression was bleak. 'I don't know that management will see it that way. If they find that I was negligent, that will be the end of my career, the end of all that I've worked for.'

'I don't think it will be as dramatic as that.' Surely, at worst it would be a black mark on his record? That could stop him from getting promotion, or even prevent him from obtaining the kind of jobs that he wanted, but it wouldn't stop him from practising medicine, would it? 'I know that it looks bad right now, but we could sit down and think things through, and work out what you have to say. I'll back you up.'

'You're a good friend to me.' He looked at her and there was a sad smile in his eyes. 'I know that you'll do everything that you can, but in the end it all comes down to proof, and I simply don't have any. When all's said and done, a patient nearly died. His relatives have every right to ask for an inquiry.'

'But you apologised to them for what happened, didn't you? And even more importantly, you apologised to the patient. I know you went to see the wife and brother afterwards. You didn't try to hide anything. It was a genuine accident. Surely, even though they are upset, they can understand that.'

He shook his head. 'They think it shouldn't have happened in the first place, and they're right. I believe that I did everything that I should to prevent something like that happening, but all the evidence shows that the pump was put back into action, and I'm responsible for that. It makes me look as though I don't care, and if I could be slapdash in that area, then I would fall under suspicion for other things. Any time anything went wrong, the finger would point at me.'

He went over to the table and slumped down in a chair. 'I can scarcely believe that this is happening to me. It's like a bad dream.' He stared into space. 'It's taken a lot for me to get where I am. It's been a struggle right from the start. I wasn't one of the usual young candidates applying for a place at medical school. I was older, around twenty-six, when I decided that I wanted a change of career. That made it all the more difficult, but I managed to persuade the interview board that I had what it took to become a successful doctor. And then I had to prove myself against all those bright young people who were coming straight out of school.'

She touched his hand, and he looked up at her. 'You did it, though,' she said. 'You made the grade, and you're a good doctor. I've seen you at work, and I know it. I think Nick realises it, too. He'll put in a good word for you, won't he?'

Casey's mouth made a straight line. 'I don't know. I don't know what he's thinking. He said that he was going to look through my employment records and gather character references, and I'm presuming that he's going to add those to his own. I would have hoped that he hadn't needed them.'

Amber was thoughtful. 'I imagine he must be thinking that anything will be a bonus when it's added to the statements.' It sounded as though Nick was at least doing something to help. She glanced up at him. 'You were with the lifeboat service, weren't you?'

'That's right. I've always been used to the outdoor life and it seemed a logical step to take. I was with the armed services for a while before I trained to be a doctor, and it taught me to be self-sufficient and pro-active. I saw wounded men being treated by the medical corps, and it made me realise that there was something else I wanted to do, something where I could make a difference. It became more important to me than anything else. All I wanted to do after that was to become a doctor.' He pressed his lips together. 'Now it seems as though it has all been for nothing.'

Amber was trying to take in everything that he was saying. This was the first time she had known anything of his earlier background. Could it be a coincidence that some of it mirrored her brother's?

Mandy put her head round the door and said, 'We need you out here right away, Amber. The paramedics are bringing in some people who were injured in a fall. There are multiple fractures and internal injuries.'

Amber stood up. 'I'm on my way.' She looked at Casey, and rested a hand lightly on his shoulder. 'You mustn't look on the black side,' she told him. 'We'll find a way through this. I'll talk to Nick, and I'm sure that we'll come up with something.'

Over and over in her mind, as she went to tend to the injured people, it kept coming back to her what he had said about his life as a soldier. Was it possible that he had simply chosen a similar path to that of her brother? They were of a similar age. Could he and her brother be one and the same? The thought lanced through her mind.

How could it be? Her brother was Kyle, and he was Casey, but they did share the same surname. It was a common surname, and that was why she had thought nothing of it before. She had always thought that her brother would have her surname, but her father had never adopted Kyle, and although at school Kyle had used his stepfather's surname in order to stop any confusion coming about because of the family name, it was possible that he had reverted to his true name after he had left home.

Right now, though, her work had to take priority, and it was some two hours before the casualties were deemed to be out of danger. Weary after her concentrated efforts to tend to them, Amber went to the washroom to change and then took five minutes break in the doctors' lounge.

Nick was already there. He glanced at her, but his expression was hooded, and she thought twice about approaching him. He looked tired, and she knew that he had been working flat out along with everyone else.

Even so, after a minute or two she said haltingly, 'I spoke to Casey earlier, and he told me that he is being suspended. Nick, I'm worried for him. Isn't there something that you could do to help him?'

He looked at her, his expression serious. 'I can tell the inquiry what his work record is, and how he has contributed to the department. I can tell them that he has always been good at his job and that I have a high opinion of his work. I'm not sure how much I can tell them about the actual incident, though. Of course, it will stand in his favour that he worked so efficiently to save the patient, and he did apologise and try to explain how the situation had come about.'

'I don't know whether that will be enough. There must be something more that you can do, surely?' She tugged at his jacket sleeve, her eyes pleading with him. 'You have to do something more for him…you have to find a way to leave him with an unblemished record.'

Nick reached for her, cupping her shoulders with his hands. 'You're overwrought, Amber. You need to calm down. I know that you want to do what you can to help him, but you have to let matters take their course.'

'Nick, you have to understand… I need to know that he's going to be all right, that he's going to come out of this with no stain on his character.' She was quiet for a moment, her breathing uneven with the force of her emotion, rasping in her chest.

She said flatly, 'I have to help him.' She glanced uncertainly at Nick. 'I think that he might be my brother.' She stopped, trying to gather her thoughts into some kind of order.

Nick looked at her oddly. 'What makes you think that?'

'It was something he said, the way he talked about his background. He's about the right age, too.'

'That doesn't have to mean anything.'

He was still holding her, and she looked up into his eyes, her expression willing him to understand. 'He said that you were going to look at his employment records, and I know that you've probably done that already. You must know something of his background. Is it true? Is he my brother? I've been searching for him for so long, and it could be that he's been here alongside me these last few months. You must know something. Tell me, Nick. Is it true?'

His hands caressed her shoulders. 'I want to help you, Amber, you must believe me, but I can't tell you what's in his records. They're confidential. They have to stay that way. If you want to know the truth, then you have to ask him.'

He drew her to him. 'I wish I could make it all come right for you. I want to be able to help, but there's a line that I can't cross. All I can say is that you must ask him yourself.'

The door to the doctors' lounge opened, and he let her go. It was a shock, that loss of contact. He had drawn her close to him as though he would shelter her from life itself. He had made her feel as though he cared, and yet in the end he had released her and put her away from him. They were still close, but for all that they might have been miles apart. It was a cold and lonely feeling.

She turned away. He wasn't going to help her. Even though it mattered to her so much that Casey might be her brother, and he might be in desperate trouble, Nick was not going to help. She had hoped for his understanding, for the warmth of his compassion, and even more, she had hoped that he would show some deeper feeling for her, a tenderness, perhaps, that would supersede all his doubts. It wasn't going to happen. He was more concerned about his position as the one in charge of the unit.

She walked out of the room and went in search of Casey. She found him clearing out his locker, and it made her sad to see him pushing his belongings into a holdall.

'Do you have to go right away?' she asked.

'Yes, I do. I'm not allowed to work until this is over.'

'Is there anything I can do? I could come over to

your place later on, when my shift ends, and we could talk. We might remember something about the first incident with the pump. Perhaps there were other witnesses as to what happened. They might recall what steps you took to arrange for its removal.'

'I've racked my brain trying to think what else I can do,' he said. 'I haven't come up with anything.' He glanced at her. 'Thank you for standing by me.'

'Casey,' she said softly, 'there's something else. I have to ask you this... I need to know, so please forgive me for asking...'

'What is it?'

'Are you my brother? Is it possible that you're my half-brother, that you walked away from us all those years ago?'

He stopped what he was doing and turned to look at her. He pulled in a deep breath and then let it slowly out again. 'I wondered if you would realise the truth,' he said quietly. His shoulders slumped. 'I've thought all along that you were my sister, because your name is so unusual, and because of one or two things that you've said.'

As he had done, she found that she needed to pull in a huge gulp of air. After all this time she had finally found him, and the knowledge made her shaky, as though the world was tilting and she was off balance. It was hard to take in.

She said huskily, 'Why are you calling yourself Casey? Why didn't you tell me right from the beginning?'

'When I was in the army, there was another lad called Kyle in my unit. Because my first names were Kyle Craig, they decided to call me K.C. and over

time it became Casey. I had the name for so long that
it was simpler in the end to go on calling myself that.'

She still couldn't comprehend that he had kept it
from her. 'But if you knew that I was your sister, why
didn't you say something? You knew that I was looking for you, didn't you? Didn't you realise how desperate I was to find you?'

'It's hard for me to explain, and I don't know
whether you can understand how it was, but you have
to try to imagine what it was like for me, leaving
home. I came to hate my stepfather. He was intolerant
and authoritative, and I could never do anything right
in his eyes, even as a small child. He made me feel
angry and rebellious. Who was he to take the place
of my father? I couldn't understand why my mother
was so subservient to him, and I think I resented her
for that. I wanted her to stand up to him, but she never
would, and I knew that things would never change.
That's when I knew that I had to get away. I felt as
though I was being swamped.'

'We hoped that you would come home, but you
never did. Mum longed to see you again. She never
forgave my father for making you turn away from us.'

There was a far-away look in his eyes. 'I did think
about it. As time went by, I wondered whether I
should get in touch, and I even went so far as to come
to the house one day. I thought my stepfather would
be out at work, but I saw him getting out of his car,
and his expression was rigid, and all the old feelings
of bitterness came back to me. I knew that I couldn't
go through with it. I didn't want the arguments to start
up again, and I couldn't face seeing the unhappiness

in my mother's eyes. Over the years it became more and more difficult to take that step.'

'I wish I had known. I wish I could have had the chance to persuade you to stay.'

'You were the one bright light in my universe. I remember you as a small child, and most of all I remember your sad eyes when I finally left. Your expression haunted me. It has haunted me all these years, and I didn't know if you would ever forgive me for leaving you behind. When I came to work here and I saw you, it took some time for me to adjust to the fact that I might have found you. I wasn't sure what to do.'

Amber reached up and hugged him close. 'I'm just so relieved to have you back. Please, don't go out of my life again.' She looked up at him. 'Will you come home with me and see Mum? She's never given up hope that she will see you again.'

He shook his head. 'I can't. Not now, not with this suspension hanging over me. I feel that I've let everyone down. I can't go back home.'

'None of that matters. We just want you with us.'

'I'm sorry, but everything has gone wrong. It isn't the right time for me to go home.'

Amber tried to persuade him. She talked to him, telling him how much they had missed him and how much they wanted him back in the family fold, but whatever she said made no difference.

'I can't come back,' he said. 'Not now.'

He finished packing his holdall and pulled the zipper. 'I'm going to go now,' he said. 'Take care of yourself, little sister.'

She wanted to go after him, but he strode briskly

along the corridor, and she knew that even if she ran
to catch up with him it would make no difference in
the end. He had made up his mind, and the only thing
that would bring him back to them was if this cloud
that hung over him were to disappear. It was up to
her to clear his name and make him realise that there
was no shame in coming back.

There were still some two hours of her shift left.
As she went to attend to her next patient, she found
that Nick was waiting for her outside one of the treatment rooms. He signed off a chart and turned to her.

'Has he gone?'

'Yes. He left just a few minutes ago.'

'Did you talk to him? Did you find out what you
wanted to know?'

'Do you think I could leave something like that?'

'And…?'

'Yes, he told me that he is my half-brother, but I
couldn't persuade him to come home with me, not
with this hanging over him.' She looked at him, her
gaze shrewd. 'You don't look surprised.'

'I had come to the same conclusion as you did. It
seemed like the obvious answer. I just wasn't sure
how he would react when you confronted him.'

'I think he was probably relieved to have it brought
out into the open. In the end, though, it hasn't made
much difference. I can't let my mother know that I've
found him, not until this business is sorted out, but
it's made me more determined to do everything I can
to make sure that he comes through this all right.'

'That might be difficult.' He frowned. 'We only
have his statement of what happened, and the facts
don't bear that out.'

'I know.' She grimaced. 'I've decided that I'm going to go and see him after work. There might be something we can think of between us that will put an end to all this.'

'I had much the same idea myself.'

Her glance shot to his face. 'You mean, you were going to see him?'

'I thought I might. Away from work, in a less fraught atmosphere, we might be able to come up with something. I've been asking him to recall what steps he took to remove the infusion pump that first time, and I'm sure there are some gaps that can be filled in.'

'Perhaps we should go and see him together.' Her lips made an odd shape. 'I'm a little afraid to leave him on his own. He seemed so downhearted.'

'I'll pick you up after work. He lives fairly close to where Chloe has her flat. It shouldn't be too difficult to find his house.'

He was true to his word. They went in separate cars to begin with, dropping her car off at the cottage, and then they went together in search of Casey's house.

'There are no lights on,' Amber said with a frown. 'I wonder if he came home and then went out again.'

'It is possible, I suppose. I'll go and check with a neighbour.'

He came back after a short time, and Amber could see that something was wrong.

'What did you find out?'

'According to the woman next door, he came home and stayed in the house for an hour or so. Then she saw him as he was coming down the front path, and he said he was off to the shops to pick up a loaf of bread. He looked a bit depressed, she said, and she asked him if he had eaten yet, and he said he hadn't. She's suggested that he come around and have supper with her and her husband, and apparently he agreed. He was going to pick up some sugar for her from the store, and she was expecting him back from there some twenty minutes ago. It seems odd that he would make that arrangement and then not keep to it.'

Amber's brows drew together. 'His car is here, so he must have walked. Perhaps we should wander over to the store and see if anything is keeping him? It will give us a chance to talk to him on the way back. If he's going to his neighbour's house he won't want us hanging around, will he?'

'That's fine by me. The woman said the store is over in that direction.' He led the way, following the route that the neighbour had indicated.

The streets were relatively empty at this time of the evening, and Amber guessed that most people would be at home, making preparations for the evening meal. At least Casey, or Kyle, was not so depressed by events that he was going to let things get on top of him. Accepting his neighbour's invitation had been a good thing to do and she was glad for him.

'Amber, do you see that?'

Amber stopped walking and looked at Nick. 'I don't see anything,' she said, 'except this walkway alongside the common and the houses in the distance. We can't be far from the store now, can we?'

'Look over there,' he said, and she let her gaze travel where he was pointing.

'Do you mean that grey sack next to the shrubbery?' she asked. 'I don't know why people tip rubbish away like that. They obviously don't care about the environment.'

Nick began to walk towards the sack, and Amber frowned and then hurried after him. 'I don't think it is a sack,' Nick said. 'Wasn't Casey wearing a grey T-shirt?'

Amber felt a trickle of ice run along her spine. 'You're right,' she said. Then, as she saw the outline of a crumpled body, she whispered, 'Oh, no… What's happened? Do you think he's hurt? Perhaps he simply fell.'

Nick was already kneeling down beside Casey's still form. He was curled up, with his back towards them. 'I'm afraid it's worse than that,' Nick said. 'He's been stabbed.' He pulled his phone from his pocket and called the emergency services.

Amber's eyes widened in disbelief. 'Stabbed?' She got down on her knees beside her brother and saw the blood seeping from a wound to his abdomen. 'I need something to stem the flow,' she said. Making a split-second decision, she wriggled out of her cotton half-slip and folded it up, making a wad of it. She began to apply pressure to the wound.

'Will you stay with him?' Nick said. 'I'm going to run back to the car and get my emergency bag.'

'Yes, go…quickly.' She took off her jacket and laid it over Casey. He was slipping into shock, and she felt helpless.

He had lost a lot of blood, and he was barely conscious, but she spoke to him gently and tried to reassure him. 'The ambulance is on its way. We'll take care of you.'

He mumbled something, and she leaned closer to him trying to catch what he was trying to say. 'How did it happen?' she asked.

His lips moved, and she thought she made out the words 'burglary' and 'chase' but the rest was indistinct.

She prayed for Nick to get back. It looked as though her brother had a knife wound to his liver, but she didn't know what other damage might have been done.

What was the hold-up with the ambulance? She looked around, and she listened, but there was no sight or sound of it.

'How is he doing?' Nick came and crouched down beside her.

'He's lost a lot of blood. He keeps slipping in and out of consciousness.'

'Let's get some fluids into him. I've brought a bag of saline.'

At last the ambulance siren sounded in the distance, and Nick went to direct the paramedics to the casualty.

'I'll go with him in the ambulance,' Amber said.

Nick nodded. 'I'll follow in my car.'

She glanced at him. 'You don't have to.' This wasn't his brother after all.

His eyes darkened. 'I know, but I will, all the same.'

The journey to the hospital seemed endless, although it probably only took ten minutes or so. The team on duty took charge as soon as Casey was wheeled into A and E, and by the time Nick arrived, he was already on his way up to Theatre.

Amber was in the relatives' waiting room. It was more private in there than the doctors' lounge would have been, and she didn't want anyone to witness her grief.

Nick came over to her and put his arms around her. 'The surgeon will take good care of him,' he told her. 'He's hoping that he'll be able to save his liver.'

'How can this be happening?' she asked, looking up at him with tear-drenched eyes. 'I've only just found him. How can he be taken from me just as I have him back?'

Nick's hand stroked the back of her head, his fingers tangling with her silky curls. 'Try not to fret so,' he murmured. 'We got him here as quickly as we could, and the surgeon is a good man. He'll do everything he can.'

'But he lost so much blood.' Amber began to weep, soft, silent tears that ran down her cheeks. Nick brushed them away with his fingers, and then he leaned closer and kissed her trembling mouth. 'Lean on me,' he said softly, against her lips. 'Let me take your pain away.'

He kissed her again and held her tightly, as though he would never let her go, and Amber rested her head against his shoulder, glad that Nick was by her side in her hour of need.

If only she could count on him to be there through all her troubles. Was it possible? If Casey came through this, would Nick still be there to champion their cause? Could she trust him?

CHAPTER EIGHT

'YOU should try to eat something,' Nick said. 'It could be a while before we hear any news.' He put a tray down on the small table in the waiting room, and inspected the packages he had bought. 'There are salad sandwiches, and cheese, and I brought some coffee as well.'

'I'll have some of the coffee, thanks.' Amber didn't feel like eating, but she was thirsty, and she sipped at the hot liquid as though it had lifesaving qualities.

'I'm sorry I was away so long,' Nick said. 'I tried to hurry back to you, but the police officers who came to investigate caught up with me and insisted on asking me some questions. How are you bearing up?' He was watching her closely, and she tried to brace herself against the uncertainty she was feeling inside.

'I'll be fine. I just need to know that Casey's going to pull through.'

He came and sat next to her and she was glad of his nearness. It was as though just by having him close some of his strength might seep into her. They were silent for a while, sipping coffee, and then he asked, 'Have you thought again about letting your mother know who he really is?'

'So that she can be by his side, you mean?' Amber's brow furrowed. 'Deep inside, I know that's what I should do. I know that it would be better if she could be here, to be with him when he comes round from the anaesthetic, because if he doesn't come out of this she has lost him for ever, hasn't she? Then I would feel so guilty.'

She put her cup down on the table and stared at her hands. 'It isn't as simple as that, though. Casey told me that he didn't want to see her yet—not until he had cleared himself. While he's under a cloud, he wants things to stay the way they are.'

'Perhaps circumstances have changed all that.'

'I don't know. Besides…' She broke off, debating within herself what she ought to do. She looked up at him, and she knew that her eyes must show the strain of everything that she was going through, but she couldn't hide her anguish. 'I'm not sure that my mother is well enough to go through all this. Her headaches have been getting worse lately, and I'm beginning to be really worried that something is badly wrong. I'm just afraid that the shock could tip her over into something much worse.'

Nick slid an arm around her. 'She's due to see the specialist very soon, isn't she?'

Amber made a rueful face. 'Today. Her appointment was for today—well, this afternoon.' She was losing track of time, but when she glanced up at the window, she could see that outside it was dark, and she recalled that these were still the early hours of the morning. 'They fitted her with a monitor, and it showed that her blood pressure is high all the time. Aunt Rose rang me to say that the neurologist looked at the results and said he would see her right away.'

The door to the waiting room opened, and Amber stood up. The surgeon came into the room.

He looked first at Nick and then at Amber. 'We've

managed to bring him through the first stage,' he said quietly. 'It was a deep laceration, and we've packed the wound with rolls of gauze. We'll keep those in place for forty-eight hours, and then we'll take him back to Theatre to remove them.'

'How is he? Can I see him?'

'He was in a bad way when he was brought in, suffering from loss of blood and shock, and to be honest I believe that it was only the fact that you and Nick were able to get to him and give him lifesaving support that helped him to survive. It will be some time before we can say that he's out of danger, but he's being moved to Intensive Care as we speak. We need to make sure he is stabilised before you can see him, but I'll let you know as soon as that is possible.'

'Thank you.' It wasn't exactly what Amber wanted to hear, but at least her brother was still alive. 'Thank you for everything that you've done for him.'

'I'm just shocked that this should happen to a colleague. We all feel terrible about this.' Mr Massey frowned. 'Has there been any word as to what might have happened?'

'It's still unclear, but I had a word with the police just a few minutes ago,' Nick said. 'It appears that there was a robbery at one of the houses near where we found Casey. The place was empty, apparently, because the owners are away on holiday, but neighbours reported sounds of intruders and unusual activity. The police seem to be wondering if Casey happened across something. If he had tried to stop them, that could account for his injury.'

'We won't be able to hear his side of things for a while yet,' the surgeon said. 'It's hard to imagine what must have taken place. Obviously his attacker had no qualms about using a weapon.'

Amber sent Nick a worried glance. 'Do you think it could be the work of the same people who robbed the house near where Chloe lives? Casey's living thereabouts, isn't he?'

'It seems likely. The police said they seem to have taken the same kind of things as before:...jewellery, anything that would be easy to remove and that might have a good value attached to it.'

'I wish the police could catch whoever's responsible. It's gone beyond burglary if they're prepared to use knives.'

'It's a terrible business,' Mr Massey said. He looked down at his watch. 'I'm sorry to have to leave you, but I must go back to Theatre. I've another patient waiting. One of the nurses will come and tell you when you can go and see Casey.'

'Thanks again,' Amber said. She went and sat down, and she was silent for a few minutes, thinking things through.

'Is there anything I can get for you?' Nick asked.

'No, I don't think so. I was just wondering whether to get in touch with Casey's ex-girlfriend. He muttered her name in the ambulance, and I think perhaps she ought to be here.' She sent him a quick glance. 'I might be able to find her address, but it means looking through Casey's things back at his house.'

'That sounds like a good idea. He might keep an address book or a phone book. I could go and get that for you, if you want to stay here.'

'Are you sure you wouldn't mind?' She glanced down at the watch on her wrist. 'You're on duty in a few hours, aren't you? You ought to go home and get some sleep.'

'So should you.'

'I don't think I could rest. I want to go and sit with Casey, and perhaps, if he appears to be out of danger, I could go and lie down in one of the on-call rooms.' She didn't think that she would do that, but it wasn't fair to keep Nick here when he had to work in the morning.

'I can sort that out for you. Shall we go and fix things up now?'

He found a room for her that was near Intensive Care, and when he had made sure that she was settled next to Casey's bedside, he said, 'I'll find another chair and come and sit with you.'

Amber shook her head. 'I just want to sit here quietly on my own, and I'll feel happier if I know that you're getting some rest. I don't have to be on duty like you later today. There's nothing that you can do here.'

His brows made a dark line, and for a moment it seemed as though he was going to argue with her, but in the end he did as she suggested. 'If you need anything, just call me.'

She nodded and watched as he walked away. She sat with Casey through the rest of the night, dozing fitfully in the chair, but all the time her senses were alert for the slightest movement or sound that he might make.

In the morning, he was still unresponsive, and the nurse said, 'It's good that he's sleeping. He's been through a lot, and it will take time for him to heal. You should go and get yourself some breakfast, perhaps even go home for a while. We need to attend to him now, and the doctor will be around to look at him soon. Come back later, when you've had time to freshen up.'

'You'll ring me if anything happens?'

'Of course, but I think he'll stay much the same for a few hours yet.'

Amber left her phone number, and then took time out to do as the nurse had suggested. She went home to get a change of clothes and then she called in at Aunt Rose's house to share a light breakfast with her aunt and her mother.

'Are you ready for your appointment this afternoon?' Amber asked.

'I think so. I'm not really sure why I need to see a specialist. I was expecting to be given a few tablets, that's all.'

'It's probably just as well,' Amber said. 'At least you know that everything is being checked out. Some of these headaches you've been getting have been quite fierce, and Aunt Rose tells me that you've been having some neck pain, too. I think it's best that we find out exactly what is causing the problem.'

Her mother didn't look at all well, and later on Amber took Aunt Rose to one side and said quietly, 'I'll be at the hospital this afternoon. Will you give me a ring and let me know as soon as she has seen the specialist? I'll come and talk to both of you. Perhaps we can have tea in the cafeteria?'

'That sounds like a good idea.' Aunt Rose looked at her frowningly. 'You're not looking too good yourself this morning. You're very pale. Are you coming down with something?'

'No. I didn't get much sleep last night, that's all. I had a late night, but it doesn't matter because I'm not on duty this morning.'

'Hmm.' Aunt Rose sent her a suspicious look. She wasn't an easy woman to fool, and Amber had no doubt that she would be called on to explain at a later date.

As she pulled into the hospital car park a little later, Amber's phone rang. It was Nick, and as she heard his deep, warm voice, her heart began to thump discordantly in response. She didn't know why the sound of his voice should affect her this way, but she was glad that he had called her. It made her feel that he was close by.

'I heard that you'd gone to get a change of clothes and something to eat,' he said. 'I think that was a good idea. You needed to get away for a while. I'm sure you'll feel much better for it.'

'I do. I feel as though I'm able to think a little more clearly now. There hasn't been any change in his condition. I rang to check just a few minutes ago.' She wondered what Nick was doing. 'Are you ringing from work?'

'Yes, I am. I'm just waiting for my next patient to be brought in, and I thought I'd take the opportunity to ring you. I managed to get hold of Sarah's number. The neighbour let me into his house and I found his address book. Do you have a pen and paper handy?'

'Yes.' She reached into the glove compartment and pulled out a small notepad. 'OK. I'm ready.'

He gave her the number, and after a short time he said, 'I have to go now. I'm needed in the treatment room. I'll talk to you later.'

'Thanks for getting the number for me.'

She hoped that he would say more, but he cut the call and she sat for a moment listening to the silence. After a moment or two she pulled herself together and dialed Sarah's number.

It was a difficult conversation. Amber didn't know the young woman, and it was hard to have to tell her that the man she had been so fond of was lying in a hospital bed, seriously ill.

Clearly, Sarah was shocked by the news. She didn't tell Amber what she planned to do, and perhaps she wasn't going to do anything. After all, Casey had been the one to finish with her.

Amber went back to her brother's bedside. There hadn't been any change in the time that she had been away. 'I need you to get through this,' she said softly to him. 'I've been looking for you for a long time now, and I'm not going to lose you. I need you to be strong. I need you to get well.'

The morning dragged on, and she wished that Nick could be there with her. His shift wouldn't end until later this afternoon, though, and she guessed that he must be finding it difficult to cope with the demands of the job. He had been up most of the night and it was too much to ask of anyone that they do a full stint in A and E when they weren't up to par. It was all her fault.

Aunt Rose rang in the mid-afternoon. A nurse came and gave Amber the message.

'She sounded a little worried,' the nurse said. 'She wants you to go and meet her in the cafeteria.'

Amber looked at her brother, and then glanced up

at the nurse. 'There's been no change for so long,' she said quietly.

'Better that than a change for the worse.'

'You're right.' Amber nodded. 'You know where to find me if you need me?'

'I do.'

Aunt Rose and her mother were sitting at a corner table by the window in the cafeteria when Amber walked in. She fetched herself a cup of coffee and handed over the money to the cashier, then went to join them. She noticed that her mother wasn't eating or drinking anything.

She looked at her mother, and straight away she knew that something was wrong. 'Has something happened?' she asked. 'Did you see the specialist?'

Aunt Rose answered. 'He was a neurologist. He asked about the headaches and the neck pain and the blood pressure, and he said that your mother needed to go and have an MRI scan. He must have thought it was important because they fitted her in right away.'

Amber frowned. That was unusual. There was a waiting list for the scanner, and if the neurologist had asked for it to be done right away, he must suspect that something was very wrong.

'I think you should tell me about it,' she said. She could see that her mother was a little shaken, and she reached out now and covered her hand with hers. 'What did they find?' She was dreading the answer, but she needed to know.

Her mother said, 'The technician wouldn't say, but he said that he would pass on the information to the neurologist right away, and that the doctor would want to talk to me again about the results. He asked me to sit and wait for a while, and then the neurologist came in and said something about angiography—I think that was the word he used. I didn't quite follow all that he said.'

Her expression faltered. 'He said I have to go to the X-ray department today and he did explain to me, but I'm still not sure about what's involved. It doesn't sound very nice at all. Can you tell me what they're looking for?'

Amber said slowly, 'It sounds as though he wants to see some X-ray pictures of the blood vessels inside your head. Usually, they'll inject a contrast medium into an artery, and that will make the artery show up on the X-ray film. Before they do that, though, they'll numb the area with a local anaesthetic, so that you shouldn't find it uncomfortable.'

Her mother frowned. 'So you don't think he's looking for a tumour?'

'I don't think so. It's more likely that he's looking for some kind of problem within the blood vessels.'

'Will you come with me? I'm a bit worried about all this. Will you stay with me? I know that I have Rose, and it's a real comfort to have her stay with me, but I'm very confused about what's going on, and you'll be able to tell me what all the technical talk means.'

Amber squeezed her mother's hand. 'Of course I'll come with you. What time do you have to be there?'

'We're supposed to go there now. I didn't want to go without seeing you first.'

'All right. We'll all go together.' Amber stood up and gave her mother a helping hand. She could see that she was unwell, and the stressful nature of the day's events couldn't be helping. 'Take your time,' she said. 'There's no rush. The X-ray department is still going to be there in half an hour's time.'

She was worried by everything that she had heard, but she didn't want to transfer any of her worries to her mother. She was already under enough of a strain. Aunt Rose had obviously guessed that this was more serious than they had first thought, and her mother must realise that, too.

When they arrived at the X-ray department, Amber handed her mother over to the doctor who was going to do the angiography. He agreed that Amber could sit in, and she sat by her mother's side and held her hand while the procedure was going on. She watched the computer monitor as the films were being taken, and she realised with a sense of growing dread what the neurologist was looking for.

It was clear from the films that her mother had a defect in one of the blood vessels inside her head. Perhaps there had always been a weakened area in the artery, but the pressure of the blood flowing through that artery had caused a ballooning, an aneurysm, which was causing pressure on the surrounding structures. The aneurysm was very much enlarged, near bursting point, and if it should split and begin to leak, the result could be fatal.

Amber was careful not to reveal any of these thoughts to her mother. When the procedure was over, she said gently, 'You need to lie back and rest now. Anaesthetics can make you feel a bit woozy.'

'Could you see what was the matter?' her mother asked.

She didn't want to lie, but at the same time she didn't want to pre-empt what the neurologist was going to say or do. 'I think there is something not quite right with one of the arteries,' she said. 'I'm not sure yet what the doctor will want to do about it, but it can be treated. I need to have a word with him, but you will need to give him permission for me to speak to him about what's wrong.'

'Of course. I'll tell him that he can tell you anything. Do you think it's serious?'

Amber said quietly, 'I think it's something that needs to be put right, and I think you should trust the neurologist on this one. He knows more about that kind of thing than I do, because he's the specialist. If I were you, I would be guided by what he says.'

It was a get-out, she knew that as she said it, but she didn't want to risk sending her mother into shock and causing another sudden surge in her blood pressure that would put even more strain on the aneurysm. 'I think he'll want to put you on some medication straight away to bring down your blood pressure. That would seem to be the sensible thing to do.'

The neurologist came to talk to them just a short time later. He was careful in the way that he outlined the situation, and she knew that he shared the same worries about exacerbating the problem.

'I think what we need to do,' he said, 'is to admit you to a ward so that we can keep an eye on your blood pressure for a while. When we feel that we have that under control, I think the next stage is to operate and clip the aneurysm. That should prevent any problems in the future.'

'An operation?' Amber's mother looked shocked. 'I hadn't realised it would come to that.'

'It's important that we do the operation,' the neurologist pointed out, 'and the sooner the better.'

Her glance went to Amber. 'Do you agree? Is that what I should do?'

'Yes, Mum. I think you should have the operation.' Clipping the aneurysm would stop it from leaking and, as the neurologist had said, there should be no more problems afterwards, provided that her mother survived the operation. She didn't see that there was any other option, given that it could burst at any time.

'All right, then. If you think it's for the best.'

The neurologist would explain all the risks, Amber was sure, but he would do that when her mother was in a more stable condition, when they had her blood pressure under control.

Aunt Rose went home to collect clothes and toiletries that her mother would need, and Amber went to help her mother get settled on the ward. She couldn't believe that any of this was happening. Her brother had nearly died, and now her mother was under the same threat.

'I thought I was coming here just for a straightforward hospital appointment,' her mother said, 'and now here I am in a hospital bed. It's so hard to take it all in.'

Amber felt much the same way. She wished that she could talk to Nick. She needed him. He was the one man she trusted, and she didn't know how it was that she'd come to depend on him, but right now she could think of nothing else but of seeing him and being with him.

Her mother was given medication, and before too long she was sleeping. Aunt Rose came and sat by her side, and said, 'You go off and take a break. I'll stay with your mother. I know that there are things you need to be doing. I can tell that you have a lot of things on your mind.'

Amber sent her a swift glance. Aunt Rose had always had a sort of sixth sense. 'Are you sure?'

'Yes, I'm sure. Go and do whatever you have to do.'

Amber left her with Aunt Rose and went in search of Nick. His shift should have ended just a short time ago, but if she was lucky, she might just catch up with him.

'I haven't seen him for the last half-hour,' Mandy said. 'It's been like a madhouse here. Chloe went home early, and now that I come to think of it she did ring up and ask if she could speak to Nick. She was worried about something and I think he might have gone over to her place.' She frowned. 'Tim will know. He was on duty at the desk at the time, and I expect Nick will have told him where he can be found. He always leaves word of his whereabouts in case he has to be called back in to A and E.'

Amber hesitated. Why would Chloe need to call Nick? Was something wrong with Lucy? Was she worried about the burglaries? It was possible that after all that had happened she was frightened, living so close to where Casey had been hurt. It would be only natural for her to call on Nick, wouldn't it? Besides, she might even be concerned about the inquiry and want to talk things through with him.

Then again, she might simply have wanted to see

him, and from what Mandy had said, it didn't look
as though Nick had wasted any time going to her side.

Tim was noting down a patient's name and address
and taking details for the triage nurse, but when
Amber asked him if he knew where Nick was, he
looked up and said, 'Yes, he left a short time ago. I
think he was heading over to Chloe's house. He left
me his mobile number as usual, but I expect that's
where he was going. He seemed to make up his mind
to leave here as soon as he had finished speaking to
her, at any rate.'

'Thanks.' Amber tried not to show that his answer
had disappointed her. She had hoped that she had it
all wrong, but now she moved away from the desk
feeling uncertain and alone. There was no point in
relying on Nick to be there for her.

She decided that she would go back and see Casey.
Her mother would still be sleeping, and she could be
of little use to her just now. If Casey had come round,
though, he might need someone to be by his side.

When she arrived in Intensive Care, she discovered
that someone was already with him. She was a young
woman in her early thirties, pretty, with dark hair that
fell in a cloudy mass to her shoulders. She turned as
Amber came into the room, and Amber could see that
her eyes were grey, and filled with sadness.

'Hello. Are you Sarah?' Amber asked.

The girl nodded. 'That's right. Were you the one
who called me?'

'Yes, I'm Amber.' She was glad that Sarah had
arrived. 'How is he? Is he any better?'

'The nurse says that his condition hasn't changed.
He hasn't spoken at all to anyone, apart from mum-

bling in his sleep. I just can't take it all in. He's such a strong man, and seeing him like this tears me apart.'

Amber went and sat down by the bedside. Casey looked the same as he had earlier, and the monitors surrounding him showed much the same readings as before. He was being given fluids through a drip and she knew that everything possible was being done for him, but it didn't make things any easier.

'He told me all about you,' she murmured. 'I didn't know whether you would come here to see him.'

Sarah's mouth made a rueful grimace. 'I couldn't stay away, not when I heard what had happened. I know things had changed between us, but that doesn't make any difference to how I feel about him.'

She sighed. 'I asked a friend to look after my little boy so that I could come here.' She sent Amber a quick, concerned look. 'The nurse told me what had happened to him. It's unbelievable, isn't it? The police haven't caught the person who did it, have they?'

'Not as far as I know. As I understood it, there might have been more than one person involved.' Amber frowned. 'I'm glad that you came to see him. Did you have to come far to get here?'

Sarah shook her head. 'I live about ten miles away from here. You'd think it was half the world away, because Casey hasn't been to see us in quite a while. It must be a couple of months now.'

'What went wrong? You seem to care for him very much.' It was obvious in the way that Sarah looked at him. You would have had to be blind not to see it.

Sarah's mouth made a wry shape. 'It's hard to say. I don't think I quite understood at the time. I'm still not absolutely sure that I know what was going through his head, but I think it was to do with the fact that I have a little boy. We all got on so well, and I thought that we had a future together, but in the end I think Casey was afraid that he was getting too close to us.'

'Why would that have been such a bad thing?'

Sarah shrugged. 'I had the feeling that he wasn't sure whether he could cope with being a stepfather. He said something about it not working out when it isn't your own child that you're caring for, and yet I know that he would make a really good father. Ryan loves him to bits, and he misses him so much. I know Casey tried to make it easier for us when he left, but I don't think he realised just how much he means to us.'

She looked down at Casey, and touched his hand with trembling fingers. Amber watched her without saying anything. She knew why Casey had left. He was remembering how it had been with his own step-father, and he couldn't bring himself to inflict any of that pain on this woman and her child. He probably thought he had left before he could grow too attached to them, but he was deluding himself, in much the same way as she was deceiving herself over Nick. Casey had tried to protect himself from his feelings, but it was too late for that. He was already in over his head.

Wasn't she out of her depth, too, where Nick was concerned? She remembered what he had said earlier that day. 'Call me if you need me,' he had said, and she had thought about it when she had been feeling lost and alone, sitting with her mother. But that had been before she learned that he had gone to Chloe.

He must have said the same thing to the nurse, and probably to anyone else who needed him. Amber had clung to the hope that his words had meant something, that they had been for her alone, and she had dared to believe that he perhaps cared for her enough to be there for her whenever she needed him, but it wasn't so. She was kidding herself.

He was a good man, a caring and considerate man, but she wasn't special to him. She had been wrong to put her trust in anyone. Over the years she had learned that it was far better to rely on no one but herself, and when she had strayed from that she had laid herself open to hurt.

She had no doubt that Casey had been through a similar sort of dilemma.

CHAPTER NINE

'SARAH?' Casey blinked and stared up into Sarah's eyes. A faint smile touched his lips. 'I'm dreaming, aren't I?'

'I'm here,' Sarah said. 'Just lie still. You've been very ill.'

'Have I? I don't remember?' He looked around, and there was a frown in his eyes. 'I'm in hospital?'

'That's right. Do you recall anything of what happened?' Sarah was looking worried, and Amber understood what must be going through her mind.

'I remember that Rob burnt his hands. That's why I'm here. I'm standing in for him until he is well again.' His brow furrowed. 'Something went wrong.' He turned his head slightly and focused on Amber. 'I don't know what happened to me. I know that I was in trouble and I had to clear out my locker and I went home. I don't remember anything after that.'

Sarah looked at him in puzzlement and then turned to Amber. 'He's forgotten everything that led him to be here.'

'His memory will probably come back, given time. It's likely that the shock has driven everything from his mind, but at least he remembers you and he remembers recent events. Try not to worry too much.'

Reassured in part, Sarah turned back to Casey. She held his hand between hers, and he simply looked at her without saying anything more. He seemed content just to have her near.

'I should go,' Amber said. 'I'll leave you two alone for a while. I'm so glad that you're back with us, Casey.'

He looked up at her, but she could see that he was still suffering the effects of the attack. It would be some time before he was back to his usual self, but at least he was conscious and talking to them. It was a comfort.

Her mother was still sleeping when she went back to look in on her. Aunt Rose said, 'I'm going to go back home now to try to get some sleep, but I'll be back in the morning. I think they're hoping that they can get her in for surgery in the next day or so. We just need to keep her calm.'

Amber nodded. 'I have to work tomorrow, but I'll keep looking in on her. Thanks for staying with her, Aunt Rose.'

Next morning, she checked on both her mother and Casey before she started work. Casey looked brighter than he had the day before, but he said very little, and he looked morose. Sarah must have gone home to be with her little boy, and Amber said a quick hello and asked him how he was feeling.

'It's not too bad,' he said. 'Apparently, they're going to take me back to Theatre at some point, possibly tomorrow morning.'

'After that, perhaps we can say that you will be on the mend.' Amber lightly patted his shoulder. 'I'll call in on you again this afternoon to see how you're doing.'

Her mother had reconciled herself to being in hospital. 'I'm a little nervous,' she said, 'about the operation. They say it's serious, and can't be left.'

'That's right, Mum, but you shouldn't worry about it. Just try to relax. I've brought you some magazines.'

'You're going off to work now, are you?'

'Yes, I am.'

'Tell that boss of yours I'm really happy about the way he's helped you out with the cottage, and as soon as I'm fit and well again I want him to come to dinner.'

Amber smiled. 'I'll tell him.' At least the thought of preparing for that day would give her mother something to concentrate on while she was stuck in here.

Amber left her, and went back to A and E. Nick was walking with the paramedics towards the treatment room when Amber caught up with him.

'Amber, I'm glad you're here. I've been looking for you all over the place. Will you help?' he said. 'This young woman is in a coma, and we need to work quickly.'

'Of course.' They manoeuvred the trolley into place, and while Nick concentrated on protecting the woman's airway and giving her oxygen, Amber hurried to gain intravenous access. Nick made sure that she was attached to an ECG monitor, and then checked her blood glucose.

'I want blood tests for sodium and potassium,' he told the nurse attending. 'We'll do a full blood count and get an insulin level.'

'There's nothing in her notes about her being diabetic,' Amber said.

'She may not have been diagnosed yet.' He hooked up an infusion of saline, and then went to check their patient's pulse and blood pressure.

They worked as a team for half an hour or so, and Amber asked softly, 'Why were you looking for me?'

'Just to see how you were doing, really.' He glanced at her. 'I'm sorry I had to leave you. I could see that Casey was stable for the time being, but it was unfortunate that I was called away and couldn't get back to you. It was a shock to all of us, what happened to him, but I checked up and I hear he's doing much better now.'

Amber recalled that he had gone to be with Chloe. She didn't want to think about that, so she said, 'He isn't out of the woods yet, and he doesn't remember what happened.'

'No...but that should resolve itself, in time. The police are hoping to be able to jog his memory.'

'I suppose it will all come back to him before too long. Then the thought of his suspension will be worrying him as much as anything else. Is anything happening about the inquiry? Is it all being put on hold while he's ill?'

'I think management will have to hold off while he's incapacitated, but that doesn't mean we can't look into things. There might be something that we've overlooked.' He broke off to glance at the test results and then spoke to the nurse. 'We'll set up an infusion of soluble insulin. Hopefully, that will bring her around.'

Amber looked at the infusion pump. 'I hardly dare

trust these things nowadays. Did we get any information back from Engineering?'

He nodded. 'The one that Casey used was definitely faulty. It's a rare occurrence, but unfortunately it does happen on occasion that things go wrong. We need to set up protocols to guard against that happening again.'

After a while, their patient began to show signs of recovery, and they were all relieved.

Nick walked with Amber towards the desk. 'Where were you? I know it was your day off, but you weren't at home, and when I checked, you weren't with Casey. I tried calling you at your aunt's house, but no one answered. I was worried about you.'

'Were you?' She frowned. He wouldn't have been able to phone her here at the hospital. Mobiles had to be switched off because of possible interference with all the equipment, so perhaps that explained why there had been no contact.

'My mother was brought into hospital. She came for her appointment, and they decided to admit her.'

He shot her a quick glance. 'What did they find?'

'She has an aneurysm that's about ready to explode. It has to be clipped urgently.'

His expression was shocked. 'That's terrible news. I suppose the least you can say is that they managed to find it before anything untoward happened. Is she coping all right?'

'I think she's a little bewildered by everything that's happened. I'm just so glad that the neurologist picked up on it. I have you to thank for that, don't I?' Her gaze tangled with his. 'He told me that you described her symptoms and it alerted him to the possibility of something more sinister.'

'He's a good man, I'll give you that. Your mother is in the best hands possible.' He touched her arm. 'It must have been awful for you, going through all that. I'm sorry I wasn't with you.'

'It doesn't matter. I didn't expect you to be there.' It was the one thing she had wanted in all the world, but she hadn't counted on it, that was true enough.

'When does she have the operation?'

'Tomorrow, all being well.' Her mouth made a straight line. 'Weird, isn't it? My mother and my brother will be in surgery within hours of each other...and my mother still doesn't know that we've found him.'

'It has been strange all round. So many things have happened.' Nick was frowning, but very soon there was no time to talk because they were called to deal with yet another emergency.

Amber went to see Casey the following day, and managed to talk to him just before he was wheeled up to Theatre. Sarah had come to see him, and she had brought along her little boy, Ryan.

Ryan's face clouded as he watched Casey being trundled away. 'Him come back?' he said. 'Him come back, Mummy?'

Sarah cradled her son against her, stroking his hair and murmuring soothing words. Amber guessed that she must be wondering whether they had come together again only to suffer being wrenched apart at some later date. Would Casey feel the way he had before, that he couldn't take on someone else's child?

Sarah said, 'What is this trouble that he is in? He's

been very vague about everything, but I'd really like
to know what's going on. It seems to be worrying
him enormously.'

Amber told her about the problems with the infusion pump. 'He says that he put it to one side and
labelled it and made a note that it was faulty. He is
certain that he arranged for Biomedical Engineering
to come and collect it, but that didn't happen, and it
went back into general use and consequently a patient
nearly died. The relatives are insisting that things
went wrong because of his negligence. Casey has no
way to prove that what he's saying is true.'

Sarah was quiet for a while, and Amber could see
that she was thinking things through. 'I've never
known Casey to be negligent in any way,' she said
at last. 'His work means such a lot to him, and he
always seems to me to be very thorough in whatever
he does. If he says that he followed the correct procedure, I believe him.'

'So do I, but I don't know how to verify what he
says.'

Sarah settled Ryan down at a table with some toys
that she produced from her bag. The boy played quietly, his glance going to the door every now and
again, as though he expected Casey to come through
it.

'There is something...' Sarah said, and Amber
glanced at her.

'What do you mean?'

'Well, Casey's memory is a bit hazy right now, but
if something is important to him, he usually makes
sure that he has written something down about it
somewhere...a sort of log of the incident, if you like.'

'I think Nick has already checked the logbook,' Amber said, 'but I can check again, just in case.' She sent Sarah a swift smile. 'Thanks for that. It's a start, anyway. Perhaps I can look through some of Casey's papers. There might be something we can use.'

Casey came back from Theatre some time later, but he was still groggy, and Amber left him with Sarah after satisfying herself that he was in reasonable shape. 'I have to go,' she told Sarah. 'My mother's having surgery soon, and I need to be there.'

She was with her mother when she was taken up to Theatre. It was a nerve-racking time for both her and Aunt Rose, and they sat in the waiting room, talking quietly or pacing the floor.

'Can I get anything for either of you?' Amber was startled to see Nick come into the room.

'Not for me, thanks.' She sent him a fleeting glance. He was wearing dark grey trousers that were beautifully cut, and his shirt was crisp and fresh. His tie was subdued, but blended perfectly with his shirt. It was odd that she should notice such things at a time like this, but he looked good, as always, and it cheered her to see him.

She turned to Aunt Rose. 'This is my boss, Nick Bradburn. You've heard a lot about him, haven't you?'

'I certainly have. Amber's mother has never met you, but she's always singing your praises.'

Looking back at Nick, Amber said, 'You know, my mother is desperate to meet you. She wants to invite you to dinner when she's back on her feet. It's to thank you for all that you've done for me back at the cottage.' She didn't tell him about her mother's matchmaking ideas. Her mother was a dreamer, and that would be one step too far.

'I'd like that.' His mouth curved in a smile. 'It isn't necessary to thank me, but I'd enjoy spending time with your mother and your aunt, and a home-cooked meal would be delicious, I'm sure.'

He went and fetched coffee, and they all sat and waited for news. It was a long time coming, and Amber was getting more and more distracted by the minute.

He came and sat next to her and covered her restless hands with his own. 'She'll come through this, I'm sure of it.'

Amber lowered her voice. She wasn't sure how much Aunt Rose knew about the dangers of the operation. 'I shan't be happy until I know that she's in Recovery and that all her responses are what they should be.'

'That could be a while,' Nick said. 'It could take a day or so before we know that all is well. Perhaps you should take things one step at a time?'

'I'll try.' Changing the subject, she asked, 'How are you getting on with the inquiry? Have you managed to find out anything new?'

'Only that Tim confirmed that Chloe had asked him to call Biomedical Engineering to send someone to come and collect the pump. Apparently, they came, but no pump had been left for them, so they assumed it had been collected by another agency.'

Amber's brow indented. 'So we're back where we started. People will still assume that Casey neglected to put it to one side.'

'It looks that way.'

It was more than an hour later when Mr Davenport, the neurosurgeon, came to tell them the results of the operation.

'Surgery went well,' he said, 'but it will be some time before we know whether there has been any damage as a result of the operation itself. We are keeping your mother in Intensive Care, and of course everything possible will be done to make her comfortable. You have to be patient for a day or so, and hope for the best. These things are always tricky, but I can tell you that things went as well as we had hoped.'

'Thank you.' It was what Amber had expected, but she knew that the strain of the next few days was going to be almost unbearable. Nick put an arm around her shoulders, hugging her close, and she tried to put on a brave front for Aunt Rose's sake if nothing else.

She sat with her mother for the rest of the afternoon, but by the time evening came, the nurse said, 'I think you should go home and try to get some rest. Mr Bradburn had to go, didn't he? And I know your mother's sister left a little while ago. I think she was feeling a bit overwhelmed and she needed to lie down. I'm sure the break will do her good and she'll feel fresher tomorrow. Why don't you do the same? Your mother's medication will ensure that she gets plenty of rest, and it's most unlikely that she'll come round until morning.'

'I suppose you're right.' Amber got slowly to her feet and gave her mother a tender kiss on the cheek. She walked wearily to the door. 'If she should happen to wake, will you let me know?'

'Of course.'

Amber went out into the corridor. She was surprised to see Nick unfold himself from a chair a short distance away.

'How are you?' he asked gently. 'You look tired. Are you ready to go home?'

'Yes, I'm ready. I didn't expect to see you here. Have you been waiting out here long?'

'Around twenty minutes, I'd say. My shift finished, and I wanted to see if you were all right. I didn't want to disturb you as you sat with your mother.'

'That was thoughtful of you,' she murmured.

'Have you made any plans for the rest of the evening? It worries me that you're looking so downhearted. Would you like me to follow you home and make sure that everything is all right? I know the building work is just about finished now, but you don't want to have to deal with any more problems this late in the day, do you? Perhaps I could make supper for you while you put your feet up?'

'I don't think I'll be doing much cooking at my place,' Amber said. 'The new cooker was supposed to have been installed yesterday, but I had a phone call to say that there was a delay. I'm actually quite sick of microwave meals and I don't have the energy to sort anything else out.' She glanced sideways at him. 'That makes me sound really half-hearted, doesn't it?' She tried a smile. 'I expect I'll feel better in the morning.'

'Tell you what,' he said, 'we'll go over to my place and I'll do the cooking. You'll be amazed at what I can rustle up at short notice. You don't want to be on your own, do you? Besides, you haven't seen my house yet, and if I'm going to visit with your mother and your Aunt Rose, the least you can do is come and look around my place.'

'I hardly dare look at your place after my little cottage,' she said. 'From what I've heard, your house is the envy of all the junior staff. They say that your father had a hand in finding it for you, but I don't believe a word of it. I'm pretty sure that you can handle your own shopping expeditions well enough.'

'You'd be right there. My father had absolutely no hand in my property. It was on the market, and I went to look it over and I knew straight away that this was the one for me. Come and see for yourself.'

He drove her there after they had left her car at the cottage. His house was everything that she had imagined. It was a long, rambling farmhouse, with bedrooms built under the eaves and lovely Georgian windows. Climbing plants rambled in riotous profusion over the walls.

'I'm in love with it already,' she said, 'and I've only seen the outside. How can you do this to me? I've only just got used to my little cottage and now you show me this.'

His mouth made an attractive curve. 'You know you love your little cottage, now that it's all been done up. This is much the same, only bigger.'

She gave him a wry smile and followed him inside the house. It was perfect, in every way. The rooms were big and full of light, and the furnishings were simple but tasteful. In the living room, beautiful French doors opened out onto a paved terrace, and beyond that was a lovely cottage garden, filled with plants in full bloom.

'Sit down,' he said, 'and I'll go and put the kettle on.' He led her over to the comfortable sofa and then reached down and slipped off her shoes, lifting her legs so that she could relax properly.

She glanced up at him. 'You do realise that if I get this comfortable, I probably shan't want to leave?'

'That's fine by me,' he murmured.

He went into the kitchen, coming back a short time later with a tray of tea things. 'Help yourself. I'm just whipping up a meal for us.'

She looked at him suspiciously. It wasn't long before wonderful smells of appetising meat and vegetables were coming from the kitchen, and she had no idea how he managed it in such a short time.

'It's all ready,' he said. 'I've set the table in the breakfast room. It's warm and light in there, and it's more cosy than the dining-room.'

The breakfast room was a conservatory at the back of the kitchen. The glass walls ensured that the sunlight filtered through, and the decor reflected that warmth, in pale sunshine-coloured walls and soft-hued furnishings.

The biggest surprise was the meal that he had laid out for them. In just half an hour he had conjured up a crusty meat and vegetable pie, with potatoes and succulent baby carrots in serving dishes alongside.

'How did you do this?' she asked when they were sitting opposite each other. She tasted a mouthful of the pastry and it melted on her tongue. 'It's mouth-watering,' she said. 'I can't believe that you made this yourself. It all happened too quickly.'

'Ah, well...the thing is, you see, much as I wish I could say that I'm responsible for this, I have to admit that I'm not. My mother, on the other hand, is a wonderful cook and she worries that I'm going to starve to death. She quite often decides to send food parcels my way, for which I'm very grateful.'

Amber smiled. 'I hope you'll tell her that this is the best I've ever tasted.'

'I will.' He poured her glass of wine, and they sipped and ate and chatted quietly. Afterwards, he made coffee and they went back into the living room, putting their cups down on a low table.

Nick came and sat beside her. 'There's more colour in your cheeks, now,' he said. 'I was quite worried about you earlier.'

Amber leaned back against the sofa cushions. 'I feel much better now,' she said. 'It's been an upsetting time lately, with one thing and another, and it's been hard. I asked the hospital to ring if anything should happen with my mother, so I'm hoping that no news is good news.'

'It was a difficult operation,' he said. 'It will have saved her life, though.'

'I know. I just can't wait to have her back in good health again.'

'I know that bad things have happened, but if you look at things in a different light, you have to be thankful that you've actually found your brother again after all these years. Despite all that's happened, you've been reunited.'

Amber turned to face him. 'That's true.' She was thoughtful for a moment. Then she said, 'I've been thinking a lot about the inquiry. Sarah, his girlfriend, said that he always makes a note of anything important. I haven't managed to find anything so far, but that doesn't mean that it doesn't exist.'

'I did wonder about the logbook,' he agreed. 'The pages have been pushed back so often that the spine of the book has cracked, and there may be one or two pages missing. I think we should set up a different system, with perhaps another type of log where that can't happen.'

'Do you think the same thing could have happened with the label that he says he put on the pump? Could it have been lost?'

He nodded. 'I asked the cleaners if they could recollect anything at all, and one of them did say that there was a piece of paper on the floor near where Casey said he left the pump. There would have to have been a series of errors, but it's likely that it could have become dislodged. As before, we'll have to instigate a different system so that that can't happen again.'

'In the meantime,' Amber said sadly, 'we have no evidence to put to the inquiry on Casey's behalf.'

Her shoulders slumped. Nick slid his arm around her and drew her to him. 'Try not to be too upset about it,' he said. 'We're not finished yet.'

'You mean that you're still going to try to help him?'

'Of course.' He frowned. 'Did you ever doubt that I would do my best for him?'

'I wondered.' She looked up at him. 'I wasn't sure that you were completely on his side.'

He bent his head towards her and kissed her gently on the lips. 'Have faith in me, Amber,' he said. 'I'm doing everything that I can.' The kiss gave her hope and filled her with longing. She needed him. When he was with her, his strength and support helped her to push aside all the bad things that had been happening over these last terrible few days.

His hand was at the small of her back, urging her towards him, and she went readily enough, her lips trembling with need as he kissed her once again. She closed her eyes and absorbed the full impact of that kiss. His hands stroked the length of her body, leaving a trail of warmth wherever he touched her, and with every moment that passed she knew that she wanted more, that she needed to be closer to him so that there was no space between them.

He kissed her face, running a feather-light tracery of tender kisses along her cheekbones, across her ear and downwards in a flurry of gentle caresses over her throat. A soft sigh of yearning trembled on her lips. This felt so good, so right, so perfect in every way.

'Sweetheart,' he muttered, his words a soft breath of sound against her cheek, 'I've been wanting to do that for so long.' His fingers lightly smoothed aside the buttons of the cotton top she was wearing. 'You're lovely,' he murmured. 'You're more than I ever dreamed of...' His lips found the lush curve of her breast and nestled there, before gliding to taste the sweep of her creamy flesh.

She loved the sensation of his mouth on her heated skin. He made her feel as though this was all she had ever wanted in her life, to have him touch her, taste her, show her how sweetly her body could respond. She ached for him to explore every rounded contour, just as she longed to run her fingers over the firmly muscled lines of his arms, of his hard chest.

'I never knew that I could feel like this,' she whispered. 'As though nothing matters any more. I just need to be here with you.'

'It's the same for me,' he said huskily, his hands moving over her, shaping every arch and slope with a subtle, tantalising sureness of touch.

Why had it taken so long for them to be together this way? It was all she had ever wanted. Deep down, locked away inside her, she had known that he was the only man for her. It was as though she had hardly dared admit it to herself, in case all the need and longing surged up and overwhelmed her.

Yet now, caught up in the wonder of his embrace, it seemed as though all her doubts had been for nothing. She loved him, and she wanted this more than anything in the world…except for the knowledge that her mother and her brother were out of danger.

That thought brought a cool little draught of air to intrude on her moment of bliss. She tried to edge it away, sliding her hands over his chest as though she couldn't get enough of him. Somehow, his shirt had come undone, and her fingertips encountered the silken firmness of his skin. She moved to kiss his rib cage, to trace a path over the hard wall of his chest.

He shifted position, easing her gently beneath him. 'I want you so much,' he said. 'You make me feverish, as though I'm burning up, and it's driving me out of my mind. I've tried so hard to hold back, but I'm fighting a losing battle. I need you, Amber.'

She looked up at him, her gaze cloudy with the haze of honeyed, warm sensation. 'I want you, too,' she whispered.

She wanted the feel of his body close to hers, the

strength of his arms around her and the comfort of knowing that he would keep the world at bay. Locked in his arms she could let herself believe that nothing else mattered, that he cared only for her, and he would be with her for all time.

It wasn't true, though, was it? That was the rub. He had never told her that he loved her, and she couldn't be sure that he had these feelings only for her, could she?

'Are you all right?' He was watching her expression closely, a gentle query in his eyes, and she guessed that he had sensed her sudden doubts.

'I think so. I'm not sure.'

He said cautiously, 'I meant what I said. You fill my dreams as well as my waking hours. I can't get you out of my head.'

And yet he had gone away from her as soon as Chloe had called. That was one of the things that ran like a constant theme through her consciousness. And how could she let herself get so close to someone who would allow her brother to be thrown to the wolves?

He had said he was trying to help Casey, but how was he doing that? What was he going to say to the hospital chiefs who needed to defend a possible lawsuit?

She straightened up and he eased back, letting her go. In a low voice she said, 'I've felt that way, too, but things are crowding in on me just now. It's just that so many things are happening all at once, and I can't keep track of them. I need time to think.'

'If that's what you want.' He looked at her doubtfully, but she nodded.

'I think I should go home. I'm glad that you

brought me here, but I need to get myself together. I'm sorry.'

'You don't have to be sorry about anything.' He gazed at her for a few moments longer and then he started to button up his shirt and stood up, moving away from her. 'You could stay here the night, if you wanted. No strings attached.'

'I think I need to be on my own,' she said quietly.

'All right.' He glanced at her as though to make certain that she had meant what she had said. 'I'll drive you there. Just give me a minute or two.'

He went to get his jacket, and Amber tidied herself up and looked around for her bag. Was she doing the right thing in leaving? More than anything, she wished that she could stay and put her trust in him, but it seemed as though she had a mountain to climb to do that.

All the people in her life that she cared about had gone through broken relationships, and she wanted to steer clear of that kind of heartbreak.

Her mother had been hurt badly twice in her life, and Casey was suffering in much the same way that Amber was now. He didn't know how to let himself love Sarah and her little boy, no matter how deserving they were.

Amber felt that she was in the same predicament. She daren't allow herself to love Nick.

CHAPTER TEN

OVER the next few days, she and Nick were ultra-cautious around each other. She sensed that he was watching her from time to time, but he made no attempt to intrude on her introspection.

'How is your mother getting along?' he asked one morning as they worked together to resuscitate a patient. 'I heard that she was beginning to take note of her surroundings and that there were signs she was on the road to recovery.'

'That's true,' Amber said. She smiled at him. 'It's such a relief to see that she's come through this. I was really worried that there would be some lasting damage.'

'I told you that Mr Davenport was a good man. If anyone was to get your mother through this, he would.'

They moved their patient into another room to make way for a seriously injured man. Amber glanced at the chart the paramedic handed to her and said, 'I'll call for the orthopaedic surgeon to come and take a look at him. He'll need that leg pinned.'

She went over to the phone, and when she had finished making the call, she saw that someone in a wheelchair was making his way through the door into A and E.

'Casey,' she said, hurrying over to him. 'You're getting around—I'm so glad. How are you feeling?'

'A lot better,' he said. 'The police have just told me that they've arrested two men. I gave them a description the other day when it all started to come back to me, and they said that they've had their eye on the men for a while now. When they went to the place where they live, they found a stash of stolen property. They even found the knife that had been used on me. The man who attacked me thought that he had cleaned it, but he hadn't done it well enough apparently, according to forensics.'

'So they'll be able to make a conviction stick?' He nodded, and Amber's face lit up. 'That's really good news.' She looked at him and added, 'I'd be even happier if you would go and see Mum. I can't think of anything more wonderful than you and she meeting up again after all this time.'

'I can't,' he said. 'Not until I know that I'm no longer under suspension. Maybe I'll think about it then.'

Amber was dismayed by his reaction, but they talked for a little while longer and then Sarah came to fetch him and take him back to his ward. Amber was glad that she was still coming around to see him. It made her hopeful that all wasn't lost.

She glanced around and saw that Nick had disappeared into his office. She went after him, knocking briefly on his door and putting her head around it. 'Can I come in?' she asked.

'Of course. Come and sit down.' He was working at his computer, and he said, 'I'll be with you in just a few seconds. There's something I need to check up on.'

Amber pulled up a chair and sat by his desk. She

didn't say anything, but let him get on with his work. When he finally looked up, she said, 'Management are having a meeting later today, aren't they, about Casey's suspension? I want to be able to say something on his behalf. I've typed it out. Will you make sure that it's handed to them?'

'Yes, I'll do that.'

She slipped the piece of paper onto his desk. 'I wish that there was more we could do for him. So many things seem to have gone wrong, and it was probably all accidental, but it doesn't look good for him, does it?'

'Actually,' Nick said thoughtfully, 'I think we have enough to make a good case. I haven't said anything before now because I wanted to make sure we had enough to clear him. I didn't want to get anyone's hopes up until I was certain.'

'What do you mean?' She frowned, but Nick was looking back at the computer screen, and then he tapped the printer key.

'It occurred to me that if Casey made a note of most things, he would make sure that something had been put into the computer log as well as on paper. It looks as though I was right. I've just found his entry about the original mishap with the infusion pump. We didn't find it before because the software was being updated and some of the original files were lost temporarily in the process.'

He gave a rueful smile. 'Now that I've found them again, the date shows quite clearly that he logged it in within half an hour of the problem with the pump showing up. He adds that he made a note of the entry in the paper log, too, and he gives the page number.

It coincides with one of the pages that is missing from the actual logbook.'

Amber's eyes widened. 'Is that enough to get him off the hook?'

'Possibly, because I can explain the missing pages from statements I have from other members of staff. We don't need to rely on that alone, though.

'I checked with Engineering, and they say that the pump wasn't there for them to collect, but Tim thinks it's possible that it was moved to one side when we had a delivery of equipment. He thinks the label was probably dislodged then, too, and the pump was put back into general use. Fortunately, it was only used on a couple of occasions, and there was no lasting damage in either case.'

Amber's mouth curved in a wide smile. 'So he is in the clear, isn't he? He hasn't done anything wrong, and all the facts show that.'

'That's right. I haven't been able to check the computer until now, because IT have only just finished, but I was going to go along and see Casey and have a word with him to put his mind at rest. Do you want to come with me?'

'Oh, yes. I'm desperate to see this thing through.'

'Come on, then. I'll arrange cover for us for a few minutes and we'll go and find him right away.'

Amber stood up, ready to go with him. She said, 'You know, when all this first started, I thought you might be taking Chloe's side. I wasn't sure whether you and she were involved with each other in some way. You stayed at her house one night, and then when Casey was taken into hospital she called you and you went to be with her again. I didn't know how deep your feelings for her went.'

'I would never take sides in that way.' His gaze searched her face. 'Is that why you were so cautious the other night at my house? Did you think that you weren't the only woman in my life?'

'Yes. I couldn't quite work out what was going on.'

He sent her a shrewd look. 'And you didn't ask me outright because in your experience relationships are never straightforward, are they? You have trouble believing that there is such a thing as true love, that people can be loving and trusting with each other?'

'I think that's probably right. Should I have asked you? What would you have said?'

He came and put his arms around her. 'I'd have said that I stayed that first night at Chloe's house because she was afraid. Her ex-husband had been seen in the area, and she was worried that he would come and find her. Then, when the houses close by were burgled, she was even more anxious. I couldn't in all conscience leave her. I stayed the night on the settee in the living room so that she could have a restful night's sleep.'

'Oh, I see.' Amber frowned. 'Is her ex-husband still around?'

'No, he's gone to work in Belgium. He won't be back to bother her any more.'

'So when you went to see her the other day, when she called you at work, it wasn't because of that?'

'No. She called me because Lucy was poorly. She wasn't breathing very well, and Chloe wanted me to be there to make sure that there wasn't anything seriously wrong with her. She worries about Lucy, but

I was able to reassure her that she simply needed a change of antibiotics. I made sure that the GP came and looked at her, and then I stayed until Lucy showed signs of improvement. There was nothing else to it.'

Amber didn't know how to look him in the eyes. She said, 'I'm so sorry that I doubted you. You must think I'm a terrible person.'

'I think you're a woman who needs to learn that you can trust in someone who loves you. I do love you, you know.'

She stared up at him. Her heart was thumping like a mad thing. 'Do you?'

'Oh, yes.' He smiled down at her. 'I tried to fight it, right from the beginning, but it was a losing battle. When I first saw you in that funny little nightshirt, and you were arguing with me the whole time, I knew that it was going to be hard to get you out of my mind. Then when I found that you were working here alongside me, I had to struggle with myself to keep my hands off you. I was your boss and you probably didn't care for me a jot, and then Casey came along and I thought you had a thing for him. You can't imagine the relief I felt when I found out that he was your half-brother.'

He was still holding her, tenderly watching her, and she reached up and folded her arms around his neck, her fingers gliding through the crisp silk of his hair.

'I love you,' she said. 'I wish I hadn't been such a fool the other night. I wish that I had stayed with you and believed in you.'

'Perhaps it's just as well that you didn't,' he said. 'Things might have got rapidly out of hand. I think we should do things properly and get married, don't you? That way, you'll know that I mean what I say, that I want you with me for always.'

Her mouth curved. 'I think that's a lovely idea.'

He kissed her tenderly. 'I'll take that as a yes, then?'

She returned the kiss. 'That's a definite yes.'

He took hold of her hand. 'Come on, then. We have things to do. First, we have to go and see your brother. Second, we have to persuade him to go and see your mother and, third, we have to tell them both about our plans. Aunt Rose, too, of course.'

'Of course. Aunt Rose definitely needs to know. She's a very good seamstress, you know. I might ask her if she can make my wedding dress.'

They dealt with the first matter on their list right away. Casey was stunned to learn that things were going to go his way.

'It's been such a weight bearing down on me,' he said. 'Do you think management will really accept that I'm in the clear?'

'I'm sure of it,' Nick told him. 'You'll be at the management meeting, anyway, so you will know what's said and done. I'm going to emphasise that we shouldn't have a culture of blame within the hospital. People make mistakes, accidents happen, but everyone does their best for the sake of the patients. We'll put new procedures in place to help counteract the possibility of a catalogue of errors or mishaps, and that way we should be able to prevent the same thing happening again.'

It went exactly as Nick had said. At the end of the afternoon, when their shifts ended, Nick and Casey attended the meeting, and Amber was waiting for them when they came out.

Sarah was with her, and she said, 'Tell me what happened, Casey. Don't keep me in the dark. Did they say that you can come back to work?'

'They did. Not yet, of course, because I'm just a touch incapacitated right now, but as soon as I'm well enough.' He was grinning from ear to ear and although it was difficult for him while he was in a wheelchair, he managed to put his arms around Sarah and hug her tightly. 'You know,' he said, 'I think I was wrong when I left you and Ryan behind. In fact, I'm sure of it. I behaved like an idiot.' He looked at her anxiously. 'Will you have me back?'

'As far as I was concerned, you had only gone away until you came to your senses. You have come to your senses, haven't you?' Sarah asked.

'I have. I'm nothing like my stepfather, and I know that I'll be good for you and for Ryan. I don't know why it took so long for me to realise that.'

Casey managed to look sheepish, and Sarah said, 'Well, the next thing is that you have to go and see your mother and tell her how much you've missed her, and how much you love her. Will you do that?'

'I will, if you'll tell me that you'll marry me.'

'It's a deal,' Sarah said.

Amber sent a swift glance Nick's way. There was a dancing light in his eyes. 'That will make for a double celebration, then,' he said, 'when she gets to hear our news, too. I just hope she can stand the strain.'

Casey and Sarah stared at him, and then at Amber.

'I wondered when you two would get around to that,' Casey said. 'Shall we go and see Mum now?'

An hour or so later, Amber crept quietly out of her mother's room. Casey and Sarah were sitting with her, and her mother's cheeks were flushed with pleasure. It was as though all her mother's dreams had come true in that one moment when Casey had walked in through the door and introduced himself.

She had known him straight away, and even before he had finished speaking she had lifted her arms to him and held him close. Casey had hugged her in return, and Amber had felt a lump come into her throat.

Now, leaving them together to talk quietly, Amber went in search of Nick. He had gone to fetch sandwiches for them all from the cafeteria.

'This is turning out to be a very busy day,' he said. 'I hope you're hungry. I've enough here to feed a small army.'

'I'm starving,' she said.

He put down the tray that he was holding, sliding it onto a table in a quiet annexe off the corridor. 'Me, too,' he said, reaching for her.

He kissed her, a thorough, passionate kiss that made her senses swirl and turned her limbs to cotton wool. 'I love you,' he said. 'I'm so glad that you agreed to marry me.' He paused. 'There's only one problem that I can see.'

'What's that?' Amber was baffled. She couldn't see any clouds on the horizon.

'Well, we have to decide which house we're going to live in. Yours is lovely and cosy, and you've only just finished renovating it. Mine, on the other hand, has lots of bedrooms for all those beautiful children that we're going to produce one day.' His glance moved over her face. 'What do you think?'

'Definitely lots of children,' she said.

'I meant about the house,' he said with a chuckle.

'That, too. We'll need a big house.' She gave a mock little sigh. 'I suppose that we'll just have to put mine on the market or let it out to someone.' She was thoughtful for a moment. 'I wonder if Casey and Sarah fancy living locally?'

Nick held her close to him. 'I wonder. As to you and me,' he said, his voice roughened, 'nothing matters, except that we both understand that we're going to be together for always and a day.'

'Always and a day,' she echoed.

researching the cure

The facts you need to know:

- **One woman in nine** in the United Kingdom will develop breast cancer during her lifetime.

- Each year **40,700** women are newly diagnosed with breast cancer and around **12,800** women will die from the disease. However, survival rates are improving, with on average 77 per cent of women still alive five years later.

- **Men can also suffer from breast cancer,** although currently they make up less than one per cent of all new cases of the disease.

Britain has one of the highest breast cancer death rates in the world. Breast Cancer Campaign wants to understand why and do something about it. Statistics cannot begin to describe the impact that breast cancer has on the lives of those women who are affected by it and on their families and friends.

MILLS & BOON®

**During the month of October
Harlequin Mills & Boon will donate
10p from the sale of every
Modern Romance™ series book to
help Breast Cancer Campaign
in *researching the cure*.**

Breast Cancer Campaign's scientific projects
look at improving diagnosis and treatment
of breast cancer, better understanding how
it develops and ultimately either curing the
disease or preventing it.

Do your part to help

Visit <u>www.breastcancercampaign.org</u>

And make a donation today.

researching the cure

Breast Cancer Campaign is a company limited by guarantee registered in England and
Wales. Company No. 05074725. Charity registration No. 299758.
Breast Cancer Campaign, Clifton Centre, 110 Clifton Street, London EC2A 4HT.
Tel: 020 7749 3700 Fax: 020 7749 3701 www.breastcancercampaign.org

4 FREE

BOOKS AND A SURPRISE GIFT!

We would like to take this opportunity to thank you for reading this Mills & Boon® book by offering you the chance to take FOUR more specially selected titles from the Medical Romance™ series absolutely FREE! We're also making this offer to introduce you to the benefits of the Reader Service™—

- ★ FREE home delivery
- ★ FREE gifts and competitions
- ★ FREE monthly Newsletter
- ★ Exclusive Reader Service offers
- ★ Books available before they're in the shops

Accepting these FREE books and gift places you under no obligation to buy, you may cancel at any time, even after receiving your free shipment. Simply complete your details below and return the entire page to the address below. You don't even need a stamp!

YES! Please send me 4 free Medical Romance books and a surprise gift. I understand that unless you hear from me, I will receive 6 superb new titles every month for just £2.75 each, postage and packing free. I am under no obligation to purchase any books and may cancel my subscription at any time. The free books and gift will be mine to keep in any case.

M5ZED

Ms/Mrs/Miss/Mr ....Initials ....

BLOCK CAPITALS PLEASE

Surname ....

Address ....

....

....Postcode...............................

Send this whole page to:
UK: FREEPOST CN81, Croydon, CR9 3WZ